# COUNTRY SALVATION

Y M ZACHERY

WILD DREAMS PUBLISHING

YM Zachery
A publication of Wild Dreams Publishing
Traralgon, Vic
© 2020 by YM Zachery

 Created with Vellum

# CHAPTER ONE

*P*iper opened the door to her apartment, relief flooded through her. She was glad to be home, it felt like she'd been away for far too long. Looking around her apartment she felt at peace. There truly was no place like home. For days now Piper had longed to be back in her own bed, but most of all she had been longing for her fiancé's hug, amongst other things.

Thinking of her fiancé brought a smile to her face, he was going to be surprised to see her, that was for sure. Piper had considered calling him to let him know she was coming home, but something inside stopped her, and she decided to surprise him instead.

Piper had been on an archaeological dig for the last three months and, even though they'd talked every day on the phone, something always seemed off. Talking on the phone didn't feel the same as being at home with her man. The phone didn't have that same warm, comforting feeling she got whenever he was near.

Piper smiled as she walked left the elevator and walked towards her apartment. She often wondered how she had become so lucky, her fiancé was supportive of her career and had never once tried to stop her from following her dreams. That was more than she could say about some of the relationship horror stories she had heard on digs. She remembered one woman telling her about how her husband had sold all of their belongings and moved interstate without even telling her. She had gone home to find everything gone because he could no longer handle her being away.

Thankfully Piper knew that would not be the fate of her relationship. As she put the key in the door of her apartment, Piper's mind wandered to the day her fiancé proposed, he had promised to follow her to the end of the earth on her digs, if she only promised to marry him.

With renewed excitement, Piper opened the door quietly, before closing it softly behind her. Placing her keys lightly on the bench to her left, she lowered her bag under the table. Her excitement began to build as she began tip toeing further into the apartment, she tried to keep as quiet as she could, the last thing she wanted to do was ruin the surprise.

Piper was not worried about Cameron being out, she knew he would be sleeping as it was 10:00pm and he had to get up early for work in the morning. That was one of the things she appreciated about Cameron, he was all about routine. On a weeknight, he would be in bed by 9:30pm sharp as he hated being tired at work.

Piper paused for a minute, she knew he was probably going to be a little mad that she had woken him, but her worries soon dissipated and she knew that the moment he saw her he would get over it, she knew he missed her as much as she missed him.

Piper knew that he was going to be surprised as he was not expecting her to be home for another two days, and that *had* been the plan. Piper was meant to arrive home Thursday, but they had finished the dig early and therefore had left the site earlier than expected.

Piper headed through the lounge room, towards the hall that would take her to their bedroom, taking a deep breath she took in the smells that were home. She could smell Cameron's aftershave, and the curry that he had obviously cooked for dinner. She inhaled the scent of roses that he had thoughtfully placed on the mantel for her arrival home. It was something that he did every time she went away.

Piper could not love this man anymore if she tired. Before she knew it Piper was standing at their bedroom door. Taking a deep breath she slowly and quietly turned the doorknob and opened the door slightly. She was expecting to see Cameron lying there sleeping peacefully. Her heart raced at the thought of seeing him again. It had been way too long. Facetime just didn't cut the mustard sometimes. She smiled with anticipation, she felt like a schoolgirl seeing her crush or the first time.

It wasn't hard for Piper to feel that way as her and Cameron had been high school sweethearts. He had been the most popular boy in town, and she still did not understand why he chose her from all the girls he could of had. If they had lived in the states, he would have been the jock of the school for sure.

The day he asked her to marry him had been the happiest day of Piper's life. He had gone out of his way to make it the most romantic night ever. First, he had organised her dream tour of the museum. They'd been in America at the time and she had always dreamt about going to the National Museum to see all the artefacts that had been dug up all over the world. The museum housed some of the greatest pieces ever known to Archaeologists. Cameron, knowing this, had surprised her by booking them a private tour, at night. Unbeknownst to her, he'd made sure that there was a romantic dinner set up for them, during which he proceeded to get down on one knee and confess his love.

Piper didn't hesitate to say yes, she had known that this was where her life was meant to go. And now, after more than three months of being apart from him, she was more sure of that fact, Piper couldn't wait to run a hand through his beautiful blonde hair and look into his deep blue eyes as she ravaged him with all the pent-up sexual frustration that had been a part of their lives for the last few months.

The room was dark, the only light that could be seen was the moonlight which was flooding in through the bedroom window. Piper had not opened the door the entire way, so she could not see the bed yet, but she could hear Cameron's voice.

She paused momentarily. That was strange, not only because of the time of night, but because it made no sense for him to be talking to someone in their bedroom. She could not hear what was being said as his voice was low, as though he was whispering, or had just woken up. Piper's heart and mind raced.

*Maybe he was on the phone to someone, work perhaps?*

That had to be it. But that made no sense, his work had never called him this late before.

*It's his parents. He is talking to his parents. But does that mean something is wrong? What if something had happened to her parents. Or her sister.*

As new scenarios filled her head, Piper's common sense took over. There was no need to worry about who he was talking to, it would only be minutes and she would find out for herself. Piper also knew that if anything was seriously wrong she would have herd it in his tone.

Pushing the questions out of her mind, she felt renewed happiness at seeing him now that he was awake. This was going to be such a surprise!

She smiled and a small giggle of anticipation escaped her lips as she pictured the person on the phone being forgotten once he leapt from the bed to welcome her home.

But Piper's hope fell when she drew even closer, and second voice emerged, a female voice.

*Alright a bit more confusing, why was there a female voice in her bedroom?*

She shook her head, maybe it was the TV, maybe she wasn't hearing Cameron talking at all, maybe it *was* two people on the TV. There wouldn't be any other reason for a female voice to be in her room.

Slowly Piper opened the bedroom door the rest of the way, although more cautiously than she originally planned. Something was not sitting right in her heart, and as the whole of the bedroom came into view, her world shattered.

Sprawled across the bed was Cameron completely naked with *her* best friend, Karen, who was also naked, riding him hard. Piper's mouth dropped open as she realised that it had been him talking to Karen the way he talked to Piper when they were making love.

Piper could not move, she could only stand there in shock as Cameron begged her to ride him harder, telling her that this was the best sex he'd ever had.

Piper didn't know what to do, she didn't know whether to

scream, punch them, or just kill them where they lay, fornicating in *her* bed.

*How could they have done this to her?*

This was not her life, this was the life of the people that she talked to on digs. But as the pair in front of her continued to writhe in passion, she realised that she was one of those people. While she had been away working, the two of the people that she trusted the most in her life were here carrying on, with each other no less.

Piper knew she should say something, but she was still having trouble getting her mind around what she was seeing.

*How long had this been going on. Did this happen every time she went away? Was it something new? And was this why Cameron always appeared happy for her to leave when she got a new dig to go on?*

Questions after question continued to hound her, yet she still could not move. Instead, Piper just stood there in shocked revulsion, while they continued grinding and moaning.

When her senses finally started to kick back in Piper knew she should turn away, but she found herself stuck to the floor, too horrified to move.

Like a traffic accident that she couldn't turn away from Piper watched numbly as Karen's tits bounced up and down while she rode Cameron.

And a part of Piper died inside as Karen moaned and told him to pound her harder. It was like some bad porn movie, that could not be turned off.

*This could not be happening.*

Piper closed her eyes, willing it to all be a dream. But, as she opened them, she was just in time to see Cameron flip Karen over and prepared to ride her doggy style.

It was then they both looked up and saw her standing at the door. When their eyes collided with hers, Karen screeched and tried to cover herself as Cameron pulled out of her and ran to the door trying to explain himself.

"Baby please, please, you have to listen to me!"

Piper spun around so fast that Cameron slid to a stop before he ran into her.

"Don't you baby me. You lost the right to call me that when you decided to stick your dick inside of that whore in there."

Piper flinched when Cameron reached out to grab her arm. Thankfully he knew better than to try his luck.

"Piper please, just let me explain. You owe me that."

Piper's blood boiled. She could not believe that he was standing here in front of her naked, with the smell of sex still on him, saying she owed him.

"I owe you nothing." She spat before turning on heels and heading towards the door.

Cameron followed her trying to plead his case. "I promise you Piper what you just saw as a mistake. This is the first time this has happened. We were both drunk and lonely, it will never happen again. You have to listen to me."

Piper couldn't believe he was trying pull that crap on her, especially since they had only just watched one of their friends go through the same thing. Cameron had even told her that he'd thought their friend was stupid for believing such a lame excuse.

"*Really? How does someone get so drunk that they can make such a stupid mistake?*" He had raged.

Now here he was giving her that same lame excuse. Did he think she was that bloody stupid? When Piper didn't respond to her plea he grabbed her arm to stop her from leaving.

Her skin crawled from where he touched her. Spinning around, she slapped Cameron so hard that the noise reverberated against the walls.

A small smile of satisfaction rose on her lips when her handprint formed on his face. She wanted to do more damage to his lying face, but she was not going to hang around long enough.

Piper was in no mood to hear what he had say. Just then she saw Karen coming out of the room tightening the sash of *her* robe. In that moment Piper could not be in the apartment any longer, she didn't want to hear Cameron had to say, and she certainty didn't want to hear what Karen had to say, she just wanted to get out of there.

She needed air, and she needed space.

Turning around, Piper marched towards the door. A babbling Cameron once again grabbed her arm, trying to stop her. She ripped her arm out of his grasp, but this time she didn't bother saying a word to him, she just kept on going.

Piper's mind was a jumbled mess, she didn't have a clue where she would go; she just knew that she had to get out of there. She had to leave before she did something she would regret for the rest of her life.

As she walked through the kitchen Piper grabbed her keys and her bag that she had yet to unpack and headed out of the apartment.

It wasn't long before she as back in her car. Turning the ignition on, Piper started backing out of the of the driveway, she didn't even bother to put her seat belt on. With tears streaming down her face, Piper took one last look at her home, a home that was meant to be filled with love and family. But in one afternoon all of her dreams had come crashing down around her.

Piper had just reached the end of the drive when Cameron came running out of the car park with his pants still unbuttoned, yelling at her to stop. His face was red, and he was waving his arms above his head.

But Piper didn't stop, she just kept going.

As Piper drove through the Brisbane city streets, her mind kept on playing the scene over in her mind. She was not focused on her driving and had no particular destination in mind, that was why she was surprised when she found herself at the airport.

Piper pulled over at one of the service stations that was along the road and pulled up into a car park at the far end of the lot.

She sat in the car for a few minutes, laying her had on the steering wheel, pondering her options. Piper knew that she could either go home and try and listen to what the pair had to say or head to her parents with her tail between her legs. But as Piper played those choices over in her mind, she knew that neither of them appealed to her. Piper knew in her heart that there was no point in going home, she was never going to forgive either of those lying sacks of shits for what they had ruined. As for going home to her parents, Piper was not sure that ready to talk to anyone about what happened. While she knew that she would never forgive Cameron, she was not ready for it all to be real, and Piper knew that by telling her parents about what had happened, she would be forced to deal with it.

Piper was all out of options, or so she thought.

When a plane flew overhead a new plan formed in her mind. Maybe she could use the rest of the time she had left on her Visa and really get the hell out of dodge.

Piper only needed to think about the third option for a split second before she made up her mind. It was exactly what she needed. Piper knew she needed a new life for a while, and most importantly, that new life had to be somewhere where Cameron couldn't find her. It was settled, and with a new urgency Piper made up her mind.

That was how she found herself looking at the flights leaving within the day. Piper knew she didn't have enough money in her normal account for the plane ticket, so she used the money in the account her parents had set up for her for the wedding. It wasn't like she was going to need it now anyway.

After she had booked a last-minute flight to America Piper walked over to the ATM, pulled out her bankcard and withdrew as much money as she could from their joint account. She knew she probably shouldn't take all of it, but the jackass deserved every little bit of hell she was going to put him through and, as an added bonus, Piper knew with as much money as she had on her, she could keep on the move and no one would be able to find her.

A slice of guilt ran through her as Piper thought about what her actions were going to do to her family. She knew her parents and her sister would be worried if she just disappeared without a word, and she could not do that to them.

Taking out her phone Piper shot her sister a quick text.

*Hey sis, just letting you know that I won't be around for a while. Don't worry if you can't get a hold of me straight away, I will text when I can. I can't tell you where I am going but I need you not to worry and I need you to tell Mum and Dad not to worry either. I promise I will call you as soon as I can. All I can ask is that you trust me.*

*Love you all.*

*Pips.*

. . .

After pressing send, Piper turned her phone off so that if her sister rang, she wouldn't have to deal with all of the questions, that was until she landed at least.

Piper walked to gate of the plane that would take her on her next journey, and as she sat in one of the vacant chairs, she was grateful for the fact that she still had another three months on her Visa before she would be kicked out of the country.

Piper had planned to originally be on the dig for six months when the Visa had been put through and even though her plans had changed, Piper had left it at six months in case the dig ended up going longer. For now, three months would do, after that, Piper, well time would tell. Piper would decide then what she would with the rest of her life. For now, she just needed to get out of town.

---

Thankfully, the plane boarded quickly; taking her seat, Piper buckled in and waited for the safety demonstration to happen. Thankfully she had been given a window seat, this would allow her to watch as her past was left behind and her new life began. It would also give her a sense of relief to know that she had definitely left Brisbane behind.

Casting her eyes outside the window to the black night, images of her fiancé sleeping with her best friend ran through her mind and her heart shattered into a million pieces all over again.

*How was she going to trust anyone ever again? Her fiancé and her friend?*

Piper wondered if it would have been better if the girl had been some random, upon contemplation, the answer was yes. Karen had been her friend since grade school. Piper had been with her for every milestone and heartache in her life, and this was how she had repaid that friendship. A tear rolled down Piper's cheek, and she wondered what she had ever done to deserve the heartache she was feeling.

Piper could not wait to start her new life. But she knew for sure, this one was not going to have anybody else it in.

Piper would never allow her heart to be broken again, not by anyone. That was a promise.

CHAPTER TWO

Piper had been in America for two days now, and still the memories haunted her.

When she'd arrived in Los Angeles, Piper had immediately rented a car and started her journey. She didn't have any particular destination in mind, she just knew that she was going to travel, see the world and hopefully clear her mind to a state that she could figure out what her next move was.

Her sister had been calling her non-stop since she had left the text message, her message box was almost full, but Piper still couldn't face talking to anyone just yet. She knew it wasn't fair to her sister or her parents though, so maybe tonight, when she stopped at the next town, Piper would find the balls to talk to her.

For days Piper travelled all day long, going through town after town. She would only stop for dinner and the night to get some sleep, the rest of the time she was driving. For now Piper found driving across an unknown land therapeutic. She had no place to be, and no-one waiting on her, it was freeing.

Last night she'd stayed somewhere just inside the border of California and Arizona. It was a nice little town, *Redding* she thought it was called. The people were nice, but that was no surprise. Piper was finding that, wherever she went, the minute people found out she was an Aussie, they'd ask the same questions. *Are you from*

*Australia? Do you own a kangaroo? What brings you to our lovely state?*

Piper tried to keep the conversation as light and airy as possible; she didn't want people prying, she just wanted to be left in peace. But she was the type of person that would never be rude to anyone, so she always answered them politely. Thankfully it was enough to appease them.

As Piper drove on, her GPS told her that she was coming into Colorado; she still had no idea where she was going but she would know the place to stop when she got there. And, about an hour later, she found herself pulling into a little town called Colorado Springs. Upon seeing the scenery and realising that it was getting late, Piper decided this was where she was going to stop.

Colorado Springs kind of reminded her of her favourite TV sitcom about an all-American father who lived in Colorado along with his wife and three daughters. The scenes that they had depicted throughout the show were just what she was witnessing in front of her.

In the distance, tall mountains capped with snow, towered above the town surrounded by forest. The two-story houses on the street she was currently driving down had pristine lawns and white picket fences. It was the type of place you wanted to raise your family. It was the modern daydream. *This* was the place for her to stop.

She pulled into a little B&B that was just on the outskirts of town. It looked clean, tidy and welcoming. The two-story white boarded house, with a wraparound veranda, welcomed guests. And the potted plants on each window, and the sprawling green grass of the yard in front and behind, bespoke of the happiness that this place could bring someone.

Piper parked her car in the carpark, just as the sun started to settle behind the mountains. Turning the car off she grabbed her bag from the back seat, locked the car and went to the door.

Piper let a relieved breath when she saw the open sign on the door. Turning the handle she let herself into the reception area, where a tall brunette sat behind the counter.

She smiled at Piper as she shut the door behind her.

"Afternoon. How may I help you." The young woman asked in a cheerful voice.

Piper gave a half smile as she remembered being that cheerful and happy once. She briefly wondered if she would ever be again.

Shaking that thought from her mind she walked up to the counter and placed her back by her feet.

"Yes, I was wondering if you had any room available?"

The woman smiled at her, and that smile was as warm and welcoming as the B&B.

"Yes, sweetie. We're happy to have you here. Are you new to our little part of the town?" The receptionist asked in a jovial tone as she opened the computer and began the check in process.

At Piper's nod, she continued to ask more questions. Piper was not new to this, it was the same questions she had been asked at every other place she had stopped.

"Are you in America for a holiday or are you looking to stay for a while?"

Piper took a deep breath and tried to answer the questions she herself still had no answers for.

"I'm going to stay for a while I think," Piper offered in a blasé tone.

What could she tell them? *Yeah, I just got home from an archaeological dig to find my fiancé screwing my best friend. So I decided to jump on a plane and head here with no direction or time frame in mind.*

No that didn't sound crazy or irrational at all. Most people would've just moved out of the house or gone home to their parents. What did she do instead? She left the country.

After a little more small talk, and information on things to see in the area, Piper grabbed her key and went up to her room. The room was nothing special and, much like all the others she had stayed at, it was roomy and comfortable. That was all she needed.

Shutting the door, Piper placed her bag on the duchess and then sat on her bed. She wanted to ring her sister and parents and let them know what was going on, but she didn't know how to have that conversation. What she meant to tell them, "hay yeah, I came home but now I am in America again and I don't know when I am coming home." That would go down like a lead balloon.

But Piper knew she couldn't put it off any longer, she supposed the best way was like a band-aid, just rip it off. Sighing, Piper sat on the bed and stared at the phone, planning what she wanted to say. She knew she would ring her sister first, she was the one who would be less likely to freak out.

Scrolling down through the contacts Piper selected her sister's profile. She stared at it for a few moments, trying to build up the confidence to hit dial. But she took too long, because just as she was about to dial, her sister's face appeared on her screen as the tone for *Shameless* rang through the speakers.

Piper smiled to herself. The ring tone suited Jayne; she *was* shameless. Piper really needed to be more like her carefree sister, she needed to have a thicker hide, then maybe she wouldn't have run away and left the country so melodramatically.

Shocked into unpreparedness, she let the call ring until it almost hit voicemail, but she could only imagine what her family was going through. It was unlike Piper to just pick up and leave. So, with her family in mind and before she chickened out, Piper accepted the call.

"Piper! Bloody hell! Why haven't you answered your phone? We've been ringing you for days. We have been worried that something had happened. Why would you do this to us?"

Piper winced, and pulled the phone away from her ear as her sister's shrill voice echoed through the phone. Guilt riddled her body as the pain in her sister's voice reached her.

"Jayne, settle down, you know that everything is fine, I texted you when I got here to tell you that everything was fine. I just needed space, okay." Piper tried to reason. Her family had every right to be upset with her, the text message she had left them had told them nothing.

"Piper, talk to me…what happened? We had no idea that you had even been home, then all of a sudden we get this message that you are leaving and you don't know when you will be back? That is not like you. Not to mention you left the country without even seeing us.

"How do you know I left the country?" Piper asked, shocked.

"Because, bright spark, you used the card linked to the account for your wedding to buy your ticket. Did you forget that Mum and Dad had access to it. Couple that with the text message you left telling us that you had to get out of town, we put two and two together. Mum and Dad have been frantic for the last two days wondering what the hell happened to you."

Piper felt like the worst kind of person. She loved her parents and the last thing she wanted to do was cause them any worry. "I know," Piper admitted in a small voice. She felt like she was a teenager again, getting into trouble for sneaking out of her bedroom window. She would never forget the look on their faces when she finally came home. In that moment she had promised never to cause them such pain again, but here she was breaking that promise.

"Tell them I'm sorry. I didn't mean to worry them. I'm just not ready to talk about what happened okay." She said numbly, trying to block Cameron and Karen from her mind as the images reared their ugly heads.

"Well, if you won't talk to us, at least call Cameron, he's been freaking out. He comes here every day asking if we've heard from you. Even he doesn't know where you are. What the hell, Piper? Why wouldn't you tell Cameron where you went? He's your fiancé for God's sake." Her sister's rising voice admonished.

Piper's blood boiled. *How dare he! What gave him the right to tell her parents that he had no idea why she left? What gave him the right to go to her parents place at all.*

Piper fumed and all of the anger and hurt that had been riding her these past few days spewed forward.

"You know what, Jaynie? Cameron can go to hell and he can take Karen with him!" Piper felt like screaming through the phone, but it was not her sister's fault that Cameron was such a weasel. She couldn't help the venom that entered her voice though.

"Whoah Piper, hang on, back up a bit. Please tell me what's going on." Her sister pleaded.

"Look, if I tell you what happened, you can't tell a soul."

"You know I won't," Jayne answered.

Piper was not happy with that though. "You have to promise me, like we did we were children Jayne. I need to know that you will not tell Mum and Dad."

Silence rang through the phone and Piper knew that Jayne was having trouble deciding what to do. If she made this promise there was no going back.

Piper sighed and rubbed her forehead. "Jayne, trust me when I tell you that I will tell them when I get home. Just promise me that, for now, what I am going to tell you will stay between you and me. Swear; on our bond."

Piper and Jayne had made a pact when they were younger that if they invoked the bond of sisterhood, the one who broke it would shatter their relationship for good.

"And when is that going to be, Piper? When are you going to come home?"

She knew her sister was only asking because she was worried about her, but Piper was already feeling irritated. First Jayne had ignored her plea and now she was being treated like a naughty child, she was grown-arse woman! She shouldn't have to tell anyone when she was going to come home, hell she shouldn't have even had to tell them she was going.

Piper realised that her anger was one again getting the better of her. She was not really angry that her family cared, she was irritated because she didn't even know the answer to the questions her sister was asking. Taking a deep breath Piper closed her eyes briefly and tried to get her breathing under control.

Piper knew she sounded like a petulant child as common sense found its way back into her mind. She started to think about her parents. Of course they wanted to know where she was, they were worried about her; it's what parents did. Especially since the actions of the last few days were so out of character for Piper. Piper had to give them something.

"Look, I just need space. I'm not sure how long I'm going to be here. I've left my ticket open so that I can come home whenever I feel like I am ready. But for now Jayne, I don't know how long that will be. It may be a month or it may be longer depending on how long it takes me to get over this." She said glumly into the phone.

Part of Piper wanted to tell Jayne everything, but part of her was still not ready to say the words aloud. Piper new that once she acknowledge what happened it made it real, and that would mean that her perfect life was over for good.

"Piper, what happened?" Jayne asked again, quieter this time. Jayne's words hit home, and Piper could no longer keep it in. The truth just came flooding out.

"Let's just say that while I've been away, Cameron and Karen have been sharing a special kind of friendship. A friendship that I walked in on when I came home two days early." The bitterness of the words flowed over Piper's tongue and through the phone.

Jayne sucked in a breath and horror inflicted her tone, "Ohhh shit! Pipes, I'm so sorry, we didn't know. I promise. If I'd known that something was going on while you were away, I would've killed the bastard myself."

Piper smiled, surprised to find that she was feeling a little better. She hadn't realised that she had even been concerned with that. But it made sense. She wondered how many people did know, and if anyone else had been playing her for a fool.

"Look it's okay, I know you didn't know and I don't expect you to do anything. I just need space to collect myself. The only thing I need for you to do is leave it alone for now, and not say anything to Mum and Dad."

Jayne agreed. But before she could say anything else Piper added, "Jaynie, if he rings, do not tell him anything, do you understand? Do not tell him where I am, do not even mention my name, just act as if you know nothing."

There as another pause before her sister answered. "Alright, if that is what you want, that's what I'll do." Her sister said in a more subdued tone.

Piper knew it was hard for her sister to bite her tongue. Jayne had never been one to stand aside and let those she loved to get hurt.

"Thanks Jayne. Just to be on the safe side I won't tell you where I am so that you won't have to lie for me, that way he'll have no chance of finding me."

Jayne agreed that it was for the best. "How are you really doing Pipes?" She asked.

Piper thought about it for a minute. She didn't know what to say to her sister that would not add more worry. Piper simply felt numb most of the time, that was until the images started again. Then the anger and pain would rise once more.

"You should have heard his excuses Jaynie."

Tears started to fall and Piper knew she had to change the subject. "I know I worried you guys, but I have to do this for me. I hope you can understand."

Piper wiped the tears that were now flowing down her face. She knew her sister could hear that she was crying as there was a pause before her sister's voice floated over the phone.

"Okay, just please check in with us and let us know that you are okay. Send a text message, or give us a phone call at least once a day."

Piper wiped the tears once more, "that I can do." She agreed.

"At least tell me you're in one of the first world countries where I know you're not gonna end up someone else's mistress and never be able to come home." Jayne joked, half-heartedly, the concern still evident in her voice.

Piper laughed, grateful that her sister was adding a bit of levity to the mix. She was grateful that while her parents could see that she had brought a plane ticket, they could not see where she went. Piper would not put it past her sister to try an follow her to America.

"I promise I am somewhere where it is okay for me to be on my own." She offered her sister. Piper didn't know how to entirely true that was. A girl travelling around *anywhere* in the world by herself was not safe these days, but it was an experience that was for sure. Besides Piper was not stupid, she was going to enjoy the trip while she could, but she would not take any unwanted risks either. And, while she was travelling Piper hoped that she would be able to figure out what she was going to do with her life.

Piper knew she wanted to do archaeology, but she just didn't know where she was going to do it or how she was going to do it. Her biggest problem facing her though was not what she was going to do for a job, it was where she was she going to live.

Piper and Cameron had lived in their apartment for six years, but it was all under his name. Piper had been warned about not having anything in her name, but at the time she never could have predicted this would happen. Their relationship was meant to be one that lasted through the centuries.

But what had that belief gotten her, here she was practically homeless, she could not go back to her apartment, and she did not have enough money to get her own place.

That left her with one option. She would have to go home to her parents. Piper thought about how that was going to look. Here she was at twenty-five, she had nothing to her name and she was going to have to go back and live with their parents. Even she knew that was lame.

Piper didn't know what to do, usually this was where she turned to their best friend for help and advice, but she no longer had a best friend to turn to. She had no-one.

With that miserable thought, Piper knew that she needed to get off the phone, before the tears started again.

"Okay sis, I'm going to go and call it a night, hopefully I can get a good night's rest and then tomorrow I'm going to head to my next stop."

"Where are you thinking of heading?" Jayne asked, once more trying to get an answer from her.

Piper smiled. "Nice try, Jaynie. I'm not going to tell you where I am. I will tell you though that I am going to simply keep driving, seeing as much of the country as I can until I find somewhere that makes me feel like I can mend. Then, once I've mended, I will come home, I promise."

"Okay sis, sleep well and I'll talk to you tomorrow."

Piper disconnected the call, glad she'd actually talked to her sister. It made her feel a little better that someone besides herself knew what had happened. She knew her sister had her back, just as she would always have hers. Piper was thankful that there were some relationships in this world that would never change.

Piper laid down in her bed, deciding to skip dinner, again. She couldn't bring herself to eat while her emotions were in turmoil. She'd gone over the events of the last week a million times in her head.

*What had she done wrong? Why did he choose to turn to Karen? What was so special about her?*

For every question she asked, a thousand more appeared. Cameron obviously hadn't meant for his and Karen's relationship to end, but he wasn't counting on Piper finding out either. Piper knew this from the way he'd tried to worm his way out of it.

A sudden thought made Piper sit up, *shit what about Charlie?* She wondered if Charlie even knew what was going on. Charlie was Karen's fiancé.

*Was that why their relationship was on the rocks?*

For the last year whenever Piper and Karen had gone out for a girls night all Karen had done was complain that Charlie wasn't making her happy anymore. Piper had assumed it was because they both worked so hard. But now she wasn't so sure.

*Was it because she had been carrying on with Cameron?*

Piper tried to think about all the times that she had been with Karen or when Karen had come over for dinner. Had the signs been there all along, and she was just too blind to see them?

Piper buried her head in the pillow and let the tears flow. She hated that she let them hurt her like this. She didn't want to feel this pain anymore. Piper cried herself to sleep for the third night in a row; *would the pain ever stop?* she wondered, as her dreams were again filled with the nightmare her life had become.

———

WAKING THE NEXT MORNING, Piper packed her stuff, had a quick breakfast and then headed. She didn't know how far she was going to go, but she had decided that she wanted to make it to Alabama. She'd always dreamed of going there, and now seemed like the perfect time to make one of her dreams come true.

With her mind made up Piper, thanked the owners for their hospitality and made her way to the car. One inside she started the engine and plugged Alabama into the GPS; *twenty hours* it told her.

She could do that. It would take her a few more days of driving but that didn't bother her. She had no idea where in Alabama she would go once she reached there, but she had all the time in the world to make that decision. For now she would just drive.

Putting the car into reverse, she pulled out onto the road, and started to follow the GPS instructions. Piper found herself smiling for the first time in days. She was finally doing something she had always wanted to do; she had direction, and it felt good.

Cameron had promised her in High School that one day they would make it to Alabama, he knew that of all of the places in America it was her dream destination. Him promising to take her meant that he saw a future for him, a future that was no longer there. Like the rest of the lies he'd told her, Cameron had said they would make a trip of it, he explained how they would travel through New Orleans and Louisiana while they were at it. Piper had even started a savings account so that their dream could come true.

A small smile formed on her mouth. "Screw you, Cameron," she said out loud. It was her turn to take something away from him, she would live their dream trip without him.

Part of her hoped that she would find a town like the one in *Hart of Dixie*; she knew it wouldn't mend her broken heart, but at least she could figure out where her life was going.

As Piper thought about what may lay ahead, she started to think about all the maybes that lay ahead of her.

Maybe she would find peace. Maybe she would be able to get her life in order. And maybe, just maybe she would find a good country bar where she could listen to some good ole' country music, while drinking a few pints of beer, or maybe even something a bit harder.

For the first time in days, Piper felt like she had a plan and something to look forward to. She felt like happiness might just be possible in the near future.

# CHAPTER THREE

It took her three days of driving to reach a small town that finally caught her eye. Driving into the town limits, she knew it was perfect. It was not too big, yet, it was not too small either. As the saying went, it was just perfect. I was the perfect place for someone to lose themselves in.

As Piper drove through the streets she took in the ambience of the town. There were quaint cafés dotting the small laneways, a small local market that boasted the freshest products, a small post office, which doubled as a newsagent, a police station which didn't look like it would hold any criminals, a bank and, in the centre of the town was a town square, complete with a gazebo and park benches, where many of the residents were currently enjoying the afternoon sun.

There were no fast food joints, no big malls, in fact they didn't even seem to have, or need, any traffic lights. The town was perfect. The only thing missing was the alligator infested swamps of her imagination. But she could live without them.

Piper continued to drive, taking in everything around her, she was not sure where she was going to stop, There were so many delightful looking places, but nothing was grabbing her fancy. That was until she saw a sign indicating that there was a pub just outside of town that served the best grits money could buy, she knew she had to stop there for an early dinner. Piper had no idea what grits were, but she was game to try anything at this point.

Thankfully, Piper didn't have far to go before she was pulling into the carpark of a genuine Alabamian pub. Looking at the clock, she noticed that she was just in time to have an early dinner and hopefully while she was eating she could find a B&B that would have room for her for a few weeks. This was the first time she had wanted to stay anywhere longer than a night.

Piper had seen a hotel down the street that said they had vacancies, but she loved small town B&Bs, especially while travelling.

They were the most welcoming, and comforting places. She had always met the most wonderful and interesting people in B&B's

Ever since Piper stayed at a little B&B in Germany after she and her friends had rocked up at two in the morning because the ferry from Sweden had been late, they had become her go to accommodation.

Piper remembered that she had been worried that they wouldn't have a bed to stay in, but the older couple that ran the place had let them in to the comfiest beds she'd ever slept in. When they awoke in the morning, fresh ham, fresh jam and fresh baked scones were laid out for them to eat. As simple as it was, it was one of the nicest meals she'd ever had; satisfying after a long, exhausting night of travel and delays, and even though the German couple couldn't speak a word of English, she'd enjoyed their company.

Piper put the car in park and climbed out. A smile spread across her face as she walked towards the bar. The neon signs that shone through dirty windows promised all sorts of enjoyment. Piper couldn't wait to get inside and get something to eat.

Piper had second thoughts the moment she walked into the bar. It was full, people of all ages sat at the bar and in the booths enjoying the meals while discussing their daily lives.

Piper was starting to feel overwhelmed. She didn't want to talk to anyone, she'd simply been hoping that she would be able to find a quiet corner to enjoy a meal and do some research. She had been hoping that by this time in the afternoon, everyone would have been done with dinner and that the bar would have begun to empty out.

*How could a small bar like this be packed? It was like the whole town was here.*

Piper contemplated her options, but the moment her stomach grumbled she decided to just continue on with her plan. With any luck, everyone would be willing to leave a stranger alone.

Walking past a table filled with what she could only describe as true-blue Alabamian men, she made her way to the furthest booth and planted her butt in one of the comfiest seats she'd sat on in a while. The booth looked like one from a Midwest pub in the movies. The table was made of wood, as were the seats. They were however covered in a think red cushion that gave a person enough height so they didn't feel like a kid at a dinner table.

Piper looked around and had to admire the small bar. It didn't look as dingy inside as it had outside.

Outside the walls were made of wood planks, nothing unusual about that, but most of the paint was peeling and a few of the windows looked dirty, like they could use a good wash. The windows themselves were not very large. She'd almost missed the bar as the sign that stood out on the road indicating that this *was* the Bar she wanted, was missing a few lightbulbs and a chunk of the sign's corner had been smashed. The sign above the door was no better, it was only held on by a few nails and had started to wear. It reminded her of the dingy diners that were often used in horror movies, the ones with the creepy waitresses that ended up killing their customers.

It had almost been enough to give her second thoughts, but as Piper pushed through the door, all thoughts of leaving left her. Inside was the complete opposite of the outside. In here the walls were polished wood, and housed numerous fascinating pictures depicting the growth of the town. Small trinkets dotted the walls, showcasing the state of Alabama. An actual boat sat above her, spreading across two beams of the open ceiling, and the Alabama flag proudly adorned another wall. Piper was starting to learn that America was a very patriotic country. Especially in the South.

Turning her attention away from the inside of the bar, Piper pulled out her laptop and her phone. She sent a quick text to her sister, letting Jayne know that she had reached her next destination and was doing well. Piper hadn't been expecting a response so quickly, as she knew her sister was probably already at work, and as she was in the middle of her residency at the local hospital, Piper knew she was always busy.

*Sis: I ran in2 douche canoe again 2day.*

Piper smiled at her sister's new name for Cameron. She rolled her eyes at the message's chatspeak. Piper and her parents had spent years trying to train Jayne out of using the typical language used when typing, but alas, it was too ingrained in Jayne.

*Piper: Bet that was fun.*

*Sis: Do u know how much restraint I had 2 maintain not 2 punch him in the nose.*

*Piper: Please tell me you didn't let him know you were talking to me. You know that if he has even an inkling that you know where I am he will not leave you alone until you tell him.*

*Sis: No, I acted all normal and worried, like I was supposed 2. But I'm telling u Pipes it took everything I had. Karen was with him 2. She also pretended 2 be worried about u. What a biatch! I can't believe we let her in2 our home.*

All the anger that Piper had been feeling towards her best friend rushed back at the mention of the two of them together. Obviously they were still seeing each other. That told Piper so much, they both wanted their cake and eat it too. Well she wasn't going to give them the satisfaction. As far as she was concerned they were perfect for each other.

Piper looked up and saw the waitress coming over to her, so she sent her sister one last message.

*Piper: I have to go, I will call you later and talk some more.*

*Sis: Ok Pipes. Make sure U do! <3 U, stay safe.*

After putting down her phone, Piper hastily picked up the menu to decide what she wanted before the waitress arrived. The poutine caught her fancy; she'd never had that before, but she'd heard so much about it. On the last dig she had been on, a Canadian Archaeologist had regaled her with stories of skiing at Whistler in the winter. He mentioned that they had some of the best poutine there.

Right now, chips and gravy, along with whatever toppings she wanted in one bowl sounded absolutely delicious. She had thought about trying the grits, but after reading the description, Piper decided to go with what she knew. She also decided that one Jack Daniels wouldn't hurt.

After placing her order with the waitress, along with some small talk, Piper turned her attention to her computer. She had so much work to catch up, and maybe losing herself in some data was exactly what she needed.

Booting up her computer, Piper cringed as the welcome screen popped up. It was a picture of her and Cameron the day he had proposed to her; tears stung her eyes as she looked at how happy they appeared. That needed to go. If it had been a hard copy she would have burnt it right then and there.

Piper decided that before she did anything else, she would need to book a B&B for the night. She did a quick search on the Internet for a B&B close by.

A nice little place came up, and, as an added bonus, it wasn't that far out of town. It looked so peaceful, it was a farm B&B and the advertisement read that the visitors were welcome to witness the milking of the cows, and even join if they liked. Piper tried to imagine milking a cow, and giggled to herself. She had spent her life living in the city, she had never been around a cow, let alone tried to milk one. All she could see was herself sitting on a wooden stool with straw in her hair as she pulled on the cows udder. It was not a picture she had ever thought to imagine.

Shaking her head to remove the ridiculous image Piper's mind had conjured up of her in overalls milking cows by hand, she sent off a quick email to the owners, asking them if there was anything available for tonight. She had her answer within five-minutes. Thankfully they had a booking for her. She shot them a quick message saying that she would be there in about an hour and a half. That should give her plenty of time to eat her lunch and do some work. She would only worry about tonight for now. She would check with them on the morrow to see if they had anything for a longer stay.

Once that was done Piper closed the internet and was once again greeted with *the picture.* Her blood boiled as she looked at it. The picture had been taken two months ago on their holiday to Fiji. Piper wondered how Cameron could look so in love with her, knowing that he was also screwing his best friend. As she continued to look at him, Piper wondered if had had always been good a lying and what else he had lied to her about. She never saw herself as someone who was so blind to a man's faults.

Lost in her own thoughts and rage, Piper was startled when one of the men from the table she had noticed earlier approached her. Just what she needed, someone hitting on her. Piper wasn't stupid, she was what most people called a bombshell. All her life she'd had men hitting on her, and women often expected her to act like she knew it. But she wasn't like that. She was as down to earth as they came. Piper knew that beauty only lasted so long. Piper had lost many friends because the men the world would not leave her alone for five seconds.

"Hey gorgeous, how you going? You're new to town, ain't you?"

Piper groaned inside. It was always the same.

"God, could you get any cheesier? Look dude, let me stop you before you go any further. I'm not interested, okay, just go back to your table, enjoy your time with your friends and leave me alone."

For once deviating from her normally polite self, Piper put as much derision in her tone as possible. She knew she was being a bitch, but she couldn't help it. At the moment, her emotions were in turmoil and all she wanted was to be left alone. She didn't want to deal with people – especially of the male persuasion – or her problems. She just wanted to eat, work and drink; anything that would take her mind off what a mess her life had become.

She could see that he was going to say something else, and since her *'back the fuck off'* persona had not worked, she deliberately ignored him, took out her headphones, put them in, looked back at her computer, and cranked her music up to a volume that even her unwanted guest to hear. Piper had effectively let him know, in a not so subtle way, that the conversation was over. She didn't look up again to see if he got the hint, but moments later she sensed that she was alone again.

*Hallelujah for small favours!*

Putting the guy and Cameron out of her mind, she focused on her work. She had so much data to enter from her prior dig, and she knew that the professor was waiting for her report to come through.

She'd rung him when she arrived in America telling him that she'd had an emergency and would be gone for a few months. Piper had expected a million questions, but thankfully he had bought her story and was happy for her to work remotely. He had willingly and quickly sent her all the files she would need to complete the data entry.

With music ringing in her ears, and a cold drink by her side, Piper went to work, working through the piles of information they had gathered on the dig and uploading it into the database for him. It would have been easier with the samples in front of her, but they were back home; this was the best she could do.

Piper didn't know how long she'd been sitting there working, time flew when she got into her archaeological frame of mind. She could zone out for hours, lost in a sample, and right now, that was what she needed.

Piper sifted through the data for another half hour until, eventually, Piper looked up from her computer, stretched her arms above her head, and looked at the fourth empty glass on the table. Should she have another? This would be her fifth.

She looked around to gauge what the time was and realised that daylight was starting to fade. In about another half an hour it would be dark, and she didn't want to drive in the dark. Piper looked back towards the bar and noticed that most of the people had left, she must've hit the early dinner rush earlier. She looked over to the table where the guy had come from before and she was a little disappointed to see that they hadn't moved on. She would have to walk by them to get back outside.

Piper pulled her earphones out of her ears; she should probably call it quits and head out. She would work out the rest once at the B&B. The thought of the B&B made her realise that she should have checked in hours ago, she hoped that they would still be willing to give her the booking.

Piper thought to ring them, but, deciding that she would like nothing better than a hot shower, after which she would lounge on her bed and watch trashy T.V, she started packing up her computer and putting it away. She would just pray for the best.

She called the waitress over and requested the bill, and once the waitress had dropped the bill on the table, Piper pulled out her wallet and placed the money, along with a tip, on the tray and finished packing up her bag. That was when the door to the bar opened.

Normally Piper wouldn't have paid any attention to whoever entered, but her eyes were drawn to the door of their own accord as the sexiest guy she'd ever seen walked through. Cameron was good looking, but this guy put him to shame. He was the type of guy that made girls want to bed him, no matter who they were.

He had wide shoulders, and he was wearing denim jeans, a black top that rippled across his muscles and a pair of Ray-Ban sunglasses that completed the look. The ringlets of his jet-black hair curled around the collar of his shirt, giving him a boyish charm. His skin was a light coffee colour, tanned from spending days out in the sun, she guessed. He had a day's worth of scruff on his strong, square jaw and his stride was filled with confidence and swagger; he looked like he'd just walked off some runway advertising hot country boys for sale.

As she continued to study him, Piper noticed a tattoo peeking out of the sleeve of his shirt. Her heart sped up; she had always been a sucker for tattooed men. Cameron never had them – he didn't believe in marking his body, and even though Piper accepted that, she had always been slightly disappointed. There was just something about a tattoo that turned her on.

For a moment Piper was worried that she was drooling, but she couldn't take her eyes from him long enough to check. Her eyes continued to follow him as he walked to the bar, ordered a drink and then headed to his table.

He'd almost reached it when he suddenly turned his head and looked directly at her. His eyes took her breath away as they stared at each other. Her heart picked up its tempo, and she could feel the vein in her neck throbbing. Her core began to ache and for the first time since finding Cameron and Karen together, she felt lust. They were the most stunning blue she had ever seen. Damn, she could swear they sparkled like sapphires.

Piper was about to smile when someone near him spoke, capturing his attention and breaking their connection. It was then she noticed which table he had walked to. She was a little disappointed to see him join the table with the guy that had annoyed her earlier.

*Why did he have to be a part of that group of sleaze balls?*

Piper shook her head. What had she even thinking? He was part of the male population, they were all the enemy at the moment. Piper did one final look around the table, collected her remaining things, opened her bag and proceeded to shove stuff in, wiping the guy from her mind in the process.

# CHAPTER FOUR

cott walked into the bar; he needed a drink and bad. It had been a long day. After he'd finished work at his regular construction job, he had headed over to his parents' place. He'd recently agreed to do a few little things around the farm with the animals to help them out as they'd gotten older, as well as fix up the buildings as they needed it. God he didn't miss doing those chores. He and his brother had been in charge of the animals when they were younger, and there was nothing worse than waking at the crack of dawn, and looking after farm animals as a kid, especially in winter.

Drink in hand, he headed over to the table where his brother and his mates were hanging. Scott normally didn't come to the bar this early in the afternoon, but after nothing seemed to go right, his brother's invitation held appeal.

Scott was almost to the table when he felt as though someone was watching him. He turned his head slightly, looking for the source of his discomfort and found himself staring into grey eyes. Eyes that appeared as if they were full of winter snow. Eyes he had never seen before in a town where he knew everybody.

Sitting about five booths away from him, was an angel. That was the only way he could describe her as she sat there staring at him, her dirty blond hair rolled down around her shoulders in waves. It was thick with ringlets of blond curls. Then there were her eyes; a colour he had only ever seen in winter, when clouds full of snow filled the air. And her lips! They were plump and red and begged for someone to kiss her while her eyes drew him in, as if she were searching deep within his soul.

Scott was contemplating going over and talking to her when his brother suddenly caught his attention and he reluctantly pulled his gaze away.

"Don't even bother, man. She is way off the radar, even for you."

Scott glanced back at the woman, only to find her attention had gone back to what she had been doing – packing up by the looks of it. The spell broken, he snapped at his brother, a little annoyed at the loss of the connection

"What are you babbling about now, Hunter?"

"Don't worry about him," Slade said from across the table. "He's just sore that she turned him down flat when he went over to her to try his luck."

Scott's blood boiled with jealousy at the thought of any man, especially his brother touching the beauty. But realising his stupidity he took a sip of his drink and tried to focus on what his brother's friends were saying. It was hard he wanted nothing more than to go and talk to the woman in the booth.

"You should have seen it, Scotty. It was great to see him get shot down. You know how he's always claiming that he's God's gift to women and that he could get any girl he wants. Yet he couldn't even get her to look at him." Gunner added with a booming laugh.

"Look, I did you all a favour," Hunter added nonchalantly.

"How's that?" Gunner snickered.

"If I hadn't gone over there you never would have found out that she is high maintenance."

Scott shook his head, looking over at the woman one more time. She was still packing up her bag, no longer paying attention to anyone around her. He wondered if his brother was right. *Was* she high maintenance or was his brother just a tool? It *was* unusual for girls to turn his brother down, he was the charming one of the two.

Deciding to leave it, Scott sat down and started chatting with the guys. Hunter couldn't get over the fact that he had been turned down, and Scott joined in with the boys who were mocking him.

"Well maybe we should get old, *knows-how-to-win-them* here to go over and have a crack. I mean if anyone can get her to talk to them, it would be him," Hunter said, slapping Scott on the back.

"Don't be a jackass," Scott replied, distracted. He wasn't playing into his brother's game.

"What? Aren't you game? Never pegged you for a chicken!" Hunter prodded him further.

Scott simply shook his head and leaned back in his chair. His brother should have known better. Scott had never been one to bite at being called a coward. He had nothing to prove to anyone.

"Come on, I'll give you a hundred dollars if you can get her to talk to you." Hunter added.

Scott knew he shouldn't take the bet, but there was nothing better than taking a hundred bucks from your brother. All he had to do was get this chick to talk to him. Easy peasy.

"Deal," he said, shaking his brother's hand.

Scott took a sip of his beer before he stood up and made his way over to her booth. Her head was down, as she packed away more papers. He could see she had almost finished, and her bill was paid. He knew he had to work fast.

"Hello," he said, finally drawing her eyes to him. Scot was momentarily stunned by her eyes once more. This close he could see the flecks of white through them, as though snow was falling from the sky. But when she didn't say anything, he continued resolutely. "I noticed you were new in town. I hope you've enjoyed our little slice of heaven so far."

Still nothing.

"I'm Scott, pleased to meet you." He put out his hand, hoping that she would take it. When she still didn't say anything, he pulled it back and tried a different approach. "Sorry, I didn't mean to bother you, I just wanted to come over and introduce myself ..." He started to say more but was interrupted when she finally spoke.

The first thing that he noticed was that she had an accent, and this accent had the same effect on him that her eyes did. Her eyes warmed him all over and her voice resonated through him. It wasn't as high pitched as most American women's and it even had a little bit of a husky tone to it, in a downright sexy, feminine way. It took all he had to focus on her words.

"Look, I'll tell you the same thing I told your moron friend. I'm not interested, okay, so you can all just back off and leave me alone."

Scott was a little taken back by the hostility in her tone. He would have to find out what Hunter said to her, maybe he had already blundered badly and ruined Scott's chances? Hunter wasn't wrong about one thing; this chick had serious attitude. Scott knew he should probably walk away, but he wasn't one to back down from anything.

"Look, love, I wasn't trying to get into your pants or anything, if that's what you're thinking. We were just being friendly. You know, this is a friendly little town that you've come to, maybe you should pull the stick out of your ass and actually get to know the locals."

Not allowing her to come back at him with a retort, he turned around and walked back to his friends, handing over one hundred dollars to his brother. His brother burst out laughing.

"Holy crap! Not even lover boy could get her to be pleasant. She really does have problems." Hunter smirked as he held his prize in the air.

"Just forget about her, Hunter, it's not even worth going there." Scott warned as he took another sip of his beer. Even though he said the words to his brother, he knew that they were lies. The chick was definitely not from around here. When she had spoken, her accent had come through loud and clear. If he had to guess, he'd say she was Australian. Her words might've been harsh but her accent, along with her body, tightened his cock to an almost uncomfortable level – it would be well worth it if he could break down those walls.

Scott adjusted himself slightly to relieve the tension as he wondered what it would be like hearing her whisper sweet nothings in his ears while he sunk himself deep within her. It was never going to happen though. As if anyone could get through that icy exterior with the attitude she had. He didn't doubt that she was probably just as cold in bed.

He looked up once more as the girl left the bar. Scott shook his head and assumed that she would leave without another glance his way, but as she pushed through the door, she spun around and graciously flipped him and his brother the bird.

Scott laughed out loud and his friends smirked; she had spunk alright. He started to rethink his idea that she would be cold in bed. With the fire that he had just seen, he would be more inclined to bet that she would be a firecracker. But Scott's hopes were dashed when he remembered that she wasn't from here and he would most likely never see her again. Putting her out of his mind he resumed drinking with his buddies.

# CHAPTER FIVE

*P*iper took a deep breath as she walked out of the bar after flipping the loud table off. She was glad that she had finally made it out, irritated at how her evening had been interrupted. She had thought the pull to *him* had been bad enough when she'd first noticed him watching her, but when he had come over to her table, and that 'Deep South' accent of his washed over her, Piper's whole body had come alive.

It was all she could do to be rude to him and brush him off as though she had felt nothing. The feelings he invoked in her scared her. Piper hadn't felt anything like this since Cameron, and look where that had gotten her. Besides it was too early. The pain was still too raw. She wasn't ready to take the plunge with her heart again, even if only for one night. It wasn't out of loyalty to Cameron and their relationship, he had broken that the moment he had taken her friend to their bed. No, it was out of self-preservation.

As Piper walked to her car, her thoughts were once again drawn to Cameron and their relationship.

*Had she really been that in love with Cameron if she could find herself attracted to another man so quickly after their relationship had gone down the toilet?*

Piper started to think that maybe she had been the problem. Had she made Cameron feel as though he needed to find love somewhere else.

Piper berated herself for thinking like that. She had done nothing wrong. She wasn't surprised that she felt lust for another man, especially since their breakup wasn't your natural, every day go down the toilet kind of relationship. The douche bag had cheated on her and dashed any illusion of love that might have remained. It was probably normal and too easy to find others attractive right now, especially when the guy that she had thought was perfect, wasn't.

That brought her mind back to the guys inside. Piper knew she shouldn't have acted like that towards them. In fact, if her parents had seen what she had done they would have been mortified. She was normally the girl that anyone could approach. These last few weeks not counting. But today after weeks of answering ridiculous Australian questions with feigned politeness, she had reached her breaking point. She just didn't have the energy to be polite anymore.

Who could blame her? Before she'd become one of the 'statistics,' she had been the friendliest person out there. She got on with almost everyone on the digs and she had no problems flirting. But at the moment she couldn't do any of it. At the moment she hated everyone, and she felt like she had a right to be pissed with the world, especially with all the attractive, single men in it.

*They were probably all the same, they probably all thought with their dicks.*

Piper opened her boot, deposited her bag inside and slammed it shut as her mood once again headed south. She wondered if she would ever get back to being her happy self, or if this was who she was going to be from now. Was she destined to be a bitter old hag for the rest of her life? Only time would tell. Piper got into her car, pulled out of the drive, and started the twenty mile drive it would take for her to reach the B&B, where, hopefully, what was left of her day would improve.

---

BUT IT WAS NOT MEANT to be – about fifteen miles into her trip her stupid dumbarse rental car decided to break down. *Wonderful.*

Grabbing her purse, Piper thought about calling the rental company, but on realising that it would be quicker to walk to the

B&B, she locked everything up and started the five-mile hike. Surely it wouldn't be *that* hard?

Piper should know by now not to tempt fate with her words, because she hadn't gotten three minutes down the road when the skies opened up and she was drenched through within seconds.

Piper stopped and looked up at the sky. "You have to be fucking kidding me," she screamed up at the heavens.

She guessed that this was pay back for being such a bitch before. You don't mess with Karma Piper thought bitterly.

Luckily for her it was a summer rain, so it mightn't get too cold, even so the rain still made the walk for Piper uncomfortable. Her shorts and white tank top didn't give her much warmth. Piper simply pushed her wet hair over her shoulder and continued walking.

God damn it! What had she ever done to deserve this? Cameron should be the one stranded in the rain, he was the one that screwed up. Piper fumed. She was starting to get cold. "So much for the summer rain remaining warm," Piper bitched as she quickened her pace.

She had only gone another mile down the road when she heard a car coming up behind her. Soaked and miserable she was half-tempted to stick her thumb out and hitch a ride. But all of the warning her mother had given her and knowing that she was in the back woods of Alabama Piper decided she wasn't game enough to bum a ride, not as a young woman travelling on her own.

Reluctantly listening to her inner voice of reason, Piper just put her head down and kept on walking, hoping that whoever it was would keep on going. But, as luck would have it the owner of the vehicle pulled up in front of her. She couldn't see anything of the driver, just the truck. It was a Red Dodge Ram, the big badge on the side clearly recognisable. It wasn't one of the smaller ones that she was used to at home; no, this one was the American type, the kind that took up all the road. It was the kind that killers used in murder films.

Piper prayed that at least it would be another woman, but her mood instantly changed the moment the guy from the bar opened the door and pulled himself out of the car; the one with the mesmerising blue eyes and magnetic pull.

"You have to be shitting me!" Piper swore to herself. She was suddenly rethinking her stay in Satilpa Creek. *What had she done to deserve this kind of karma? Whoever was upstairs running the show was pissed, that was for sure! Maybe it was because she'd been dumping on men all day. She wouldn't be surprised if that was the case – that would be a man thing to do, wouldn't it?*

Piper stopped and waited to see what bad luck would befall her next.

"Hey there, stranger," he said, coming around the back of the car with an umbrella. Piper decided that, before she left town, she would have to make sure she had an umbrella in the car, just for such emergencies. She had to admit she was grateful that he had offered her one. Piper tried to remember his name.

"Looks like you could use a lift. Where you off to?" he asked in a friendly manner. Piper weighed her options, but she really didn't have any. She could keep walking, and get even wetter and colder, or she could accept this guy's offer. She did owe him an apology she supposed. It wasn't his fault that her ex was a total jerk.

"Well I suppose you would probably know better than me, I am heading to the Paisley B&B. Do you know where that is?" Piper waited for an answer, but instead all she got was a huge smile that spread across his face.

Curious as to his reaction, Piper was once again struck by how handsome this guy was. She liked the way his curly hair looked with water now glistening off it, curled around his face. She like the way his eyes crinkled at the corner, denoting lots of laughter. But most of all she like the way is body made hers sing.

She was starting to get irritated again. What was with her treacherous body? Why couldn't it listen to her brain? She hated men now...remember? If only her hormones would take note. Feeling flustered and confused again, Piper was just about to tell him not to bother when he spoke.

"It just so happens that I *do* know where that is." The grin that had widened didn't bode well for Piper.

"You do?"

"Yep, it is actually my parents' B&B. So I'd be more than happy to take you there. Besides, I like nothing more than helping damsels in distress." He joked, walking over to his truck and opening the door.

Piper was having second thoughts. *Why did every guy refer to women as damsels in distress?* It was as if women couldn't get by without their help, and usually they wanted something in return. That gave Piper pause. *What if this guy expected something for helping her?* Looking at his truck and then back down the road, she decided she would just keep on walking. The exercise was good for her anyway.

"Look, you don't have to help me, I can keep walking. I wouldn't want your truck to get messed up by my wet clothes. So, if you can just point me in the right direction, I will be on my way." She watched his eyebrows lift in amusement and was instantly annoyed.

"Really? You want to keep walking in this rain?" he asked.

"No, not particularly!" She snapped.

He raised his eyebrow higher at her tone. It let her know that she was once again being a bitch. His comment from the bar came rushing back to her and reluctantly she decided she *would* go with him, even if it only meant that she would soon be in the warmth of her room at the B&B and not on the side of the road with him.

"Okay, I'll go with you since you're going that way anyway." Piper reneged and stormed over to the car.

"What happened, by the way? Why are you walking in the rain? Where is your car?" he asked her as she climbed into his truck.

It was kind of high and it took her a little bit to pull herself in. She could see he wanted to help her, but her back-off attitude warned him against it. The smile on his face however told her that he knew exactly what he was doing, and that pissed her off even more.

"Well it kinda broke down," she said, pointing up the road to where her car was sitting on the side of it.

The look that shot across his face almost made her laugh, it *was* kind of funny when you thought about it.

"I know, I know, I broke a brand new hire car." she said, laughing for the first time in weeks.

He chuckled at her humour and offered her his hand.

"Hi, in case you have forgotten, I'm Scott Paisley. Pleased to meet you...Miss?"

Piper knew it was his subtle way of reminding her of her rudeness to him earlier. Although, if his smile was any indication, she'd say he was over it.

"Piper Shelton." She shook his hand.

"Let's get you out of this rain," he said as he shut her door and walked around to the driver's side.

Piper kind of felt bad about his car as she watched the water pool under her feet and around her bottom on the chair. Thankfully he had leather seats so it wouldn't be too hard to dry out.

As he climbed in, Piper had the overwhelming urge to apologies to him. Here he was being kind to her, even after her rudeness.

"Look, I'm sorry about back at the bar. I know that you were just being friendly, and I was kind of a bitch. But the guy that you were talking to at that table had already tried hitting on me."

He went to say something, but she stopped him.

"I know it's no excuse, I'm just letting you know that I'm not usually so rude, but in saying that I'm in no way looking for any kind of relationship either. I'm in a bad place at the moment and I just need time to pull myself together and find myself again. And no, I'm not saying that you were looking for one either, I'm just making sure we're on the same page. I just wanted to explain myself." Piper took a breath and looked at him. She hopes that her explanation will be enough for him and that he won't press her any further. While she told him that she wasn't wanting any relationship, she wasn't entirely sure that she would be able to deny him if he did try and come on to her. Even if it was for one night.

He raised his hands in the air as if pleading the fifth. "Message received loud and clear," he added, "but in future, how about not acting like a... let's just say... *crazed* woman." He joked.

Piper was glad for his levity. She had hoped to stay here for a few weeks and the last thing she needed to do was piss off the locals, especially the son of the people who ran the B&B that Piper was hoping to stay at. With that thought in mind she decided to play along. He was only telling the truth. After all, she had been a bitch.

"You were going to call me a bitch, weren't you."

"No *never*," He protested mockingly. "I am an Alabama boy and

Alabama boys are polite as pie, we do not call women bitches, buuuut... if the shoe fits...”

Piper laughed, it was so nice to have a conversation with someone who was not trying to hit on her. She had misjudged him and was relieved to find that she didn't mind his company. She had to admit it was a refreshing break from the dirt bags who normally tried to hit on her.

“Okay you have me, Mr. Alabama boy, now save the day and take me somewhere dry.”

He started the truck's engine and it roared to life. One thing Piper had noticed on her journey through multiple states was that America liked their big trucks, especially in the country. She sat and stared at the rain, the rest of the trip was done in silence, which suited her fine. It wasn't your uncomfortable silence, instead it was the silence one got from feeling relaxed and safe with someone. Despite only meeting this guy, she instinctively knew she was safe.

The trip didn't take long, and soon they were heading down a smooth dirt road which followed alongside a winding river. Tall trees with yellow flowers spotted the river and cows dotted the fields that lay beyond. As they came to the end of the road the B&B came into view. As they pulled up, she looked through the windshield and she was once again pleased that she'd booked this place. Thankfully the rain had slowed to a slight sprinkle and she knew soon it would be gone. While she had only been a few miles from the B&B, she was glad that Scott had stopped and picked her up. The walk down the dirt road would not have been pleasant.

Stepping out of the truck, she took in the whole picture. The huge, three-story white country-style house, with wraparound verandas and wide-open fields that stretched behind it for miles took her breath away. It reminded her of the Old Southern homes that she saw in movies like ‘*The Green Mile*’. She could easily picture herself staying here for a few weeks, breathing in the fresh country air, roaming the fields and finding herself. She wondered if she might find a special spot on the creek she could sit by and contemplate her next steps.

Remembering Scott, she found that he was standing beside her.

"Thank you for your help, Mr. Paisley. It was nice to see you again." Piper held out her hand to shake his.

"No worries, Miss Shelton. I am going to head out now, just head on in and my folks will look after you."

Piper nodded and started to make her way up the steps.

"Hey Piper."

She stopped and turned to see him standing on the running board of his truck, yelling at her over the roof.

"If you ever want to see what happens around here at night, just let me know. That is, if you wanna have some fun with no strings attached."

Not sure what he meant by that, Piper nodded at him to let him know she'd heard him. He gave her a cheeky smile before he dove into his truck, put it in reverse, and drove out of the driveway, leaving a trail of mud behind him.

Piper watched until he had disappeared, he was not at all what she first thought. At the bar she had assumed that he was like all the others, only after one thing. But her opinion was starting to change, in fact, she was all of a sudden looking forward to getting to know him a bit better. Shaking that thought from her mind Piper turned and walked the rest of the way up the stairs and entered the quaint B&B. As she opened the door, she instantly felt at home. The inside of the home was as beautiful as the outside. Winding staircases and wide open dining areas greeted her and made her feel as though she had been transported back in time. In addition to that, the delicious smell of cakes and biscuits cooking in the oven added to the warm ambiance that engulfed her, and she knew instantly that this place was going to be good for what came next.

Mending her soul.

# CHAPTER SIX

s Scott drove down the road, he couldn't help thinking back to the girl he'd just dropped off at his parents' place. He couldn't believe his luck after leaving the bar. He had just walked outside when he had received a call from his parents, worried about a guest. Usually guests showed up on time and it wasn't a hard place to find. So they'd asked him to go for a drive to see if he could find the client.

He'd briefly wondered if it would be the same out-of-towner he had a run in with at the bar, the one he had hit on, but as soon as the thought entered his mind, it left. She seemed the type that would just head on out of town. Their quaint little town would not be good enough for her.

Scott hadn't gone far when the rain started, and it wasn't much further when he saw the same woman from the bar walking down the road, soaking wet. He'd pulled over in front of her and as he'd gotten out of the car, he'd wondered what kind of reception he would get. But he didn't have to wait long, he'd taken one look at her and known it was not going to be a pleasant conversation. Not only did she appear to be cursing at the sky, and the way she held her body, with her hands fisted at her side, her body dripping wet told him that she was going to be far less friendlier than earlier.

Scott had the sudden urge to get back in his truck and drive off, but he knew that his parents would never forgive him if they lost a client to his rudeness. Even if it was deserved. With that in mind Scott pasted a smile on his lips and tried to sound as friendly and as platonic as possible. The last thing he needed was for the woman to think he was trying to hit on her again.

*"Hey there, stranger, looks like you could use a lift. Where you off to?" He was pretty sure he knew where she was going, but he needed to make sure.*

*"Well I suppose you would probably know better than me, I'm heading to the Paisley B&B. Do you know where that is?" God, she still had that tone. He was starting to think it was the only tone she knew. Maybe he should just leave her to walk in the rain. It would serve her right. But he knew he couldn't do that, his parents would kill him. Not just figuratively.*

*"It just so happens that I do know where that is." He couldn't help the smile that rose to his lips at her look. She looked as though she had just swallowed a lemon. He knew it was the last thing she wanted to hear.*

*"You do?"*

*Scott gnashed his teeth together, trying not to be a smartass. The way she had asked it led him to believe that she didn't trust him one iota. But being a single woman on a road to nowhere, he supposed he'd be suspicious too.*

*"Yep, it is actually my parents' bed and breakfast. So I'd be more than happy to take you there. Besides, I like nothing better than helping damsels in destress." He joked, walking over to his truck and opening the door for her. He was trying to put her at ease. He could tell she was having second thoughts.*

*She looked down the road and Scott thought maybe to gauge her luck with walking. He was not going to force her, he would offer her one more time, but after that he was out of here. He had a life to get back to. It didn't matter that this hellcat with her fiery temper tempted him in so many ways.*

*Her answer was given in the same snarky tone she had used at the bar. This woman's attitude was beyond a joke.*

*"Really? You want to keep walking in this rain?" he asked, not being able to let it go. He could have kicked himself.*

*"No, not particularly!" She snapped. He raised his eyebrow again, letting her know what he thought of her attitude. He thought she was going to refuse, but he took a breath when she finally agreed to go with him.*

*As she was getting in the car, he asked her what had caused her to be on the road in the rain. Upon her telling him that she had broken her hire car, he couldn't help but chuckle. She also laughed a little, but as soon as the sound was out she clammed up again. For that brief moment, he caught a glimpse of who she really was, so he decided to give her another chance. Holding out his hand he introduced himself once more.*

*"Hi, in case you have forgotten, I'm Scott Paisley, pleased to meet you... Miss?"*

*"Piper Shelton," she offered. Shaking her hand, he closed the door and walked around the other side of his truck, trying her name on his tongue. He liked it. It somehow suited her.*

THEIR DRIVE TO HIS PARENTS' place had been quiet, but he had gotten her to relax a little and let down her guard, and for some reason he had offered to show her the town. He loved listening to her accent and would love nothing more than spending his nights getting to know her. But he didn't pressure her either, he had simply left the ball in her court before he headed home.

Scott couldn't wait to get home, he needed a shower and his bed. He was beat, it had been a long day.

Once home, he showered, had something to eat and hit the hay, but sleep evaded him. As he lay in his bed, his chest bear, the fan sending a cool breeze across it, his mind wandered back to Piper. He kind of hoped that she *would* take him up on his offer to see the nightlife.

Not much happened at the bar during the day, but at night, it really went off. The owners usually had some cool country band that came to perform on the weekends, and he knew that once she had a few drinks in her she would be able to let her hair down and have a good time. Scott had a feeling that it would be during that time that he would see the real Piper. He had a feeling that the woman he met today was not her.

With his mind made up, Scott decided he'd make it his mission to go around to his parents' place tomorrow in hopes that she would warm to him, and maybe, just maybe his charm might rub off on her. He was intrigued by her and part of him wanted to be the one to break her icy exterior. He also wanted to know what had put that icy exterior there. Surely someone as young and gorgeous as she was could not have always been this angry with life.

Life had kicked her and he wanted to help heal her heart. No matter the cost.

CHAPTER SEVEN

*P*iper woke the next morning feeling fresher than she had in weeks, she knew instantly that this was going to be the place that was going to mend her soul.

She was still a little worried about the mistake she had made last night, she blamed her meeting on Scott for her absentmindedness. ,

When Piper had arrived at the B&B last night the Paisley's had asked how she was going to pay, without thinking she had pulled out her usual credit card and paid. It wasn't until she was putting it back in her purse that she had realised her mistake. The only think Piper could hope for now was that Cameron would have already checked all the accounts and upon finding nothing Piper hoped that he would not check them again.

Deciding that there was not point stressing over it now, Piper decided to forget about it and cross that bridge if she came to it, for now she wished to do nothing but enjoy the time she had, because finally she was in no rush to move on.

This little town was not like the other towns she'd pulled into. In the other towns, she had been eager to pack and get to the next one. But with this town, she had the opposite feeling. There was just something about this little town that called out to her; plus, as an added bonus, it was in Alabama, the one place on her bucket list that she wanted to visit.

After having a shower and freshening up, she decided to join the others for breakfast, something else she hadn't done in the other towns.

There was just something warm and welcoming about the people that ran this establishment.

Walking down the stairs, Piper cherished the feel of the wooden banister that slid beneath her hand, and the feel of the plush carpet underneath her feet. She felt like princess descending the winding staircase. Piper smiled at the thought. She was brought out of her musing however, when she was greeted by the same couple that had checked her in last night. Looking at them in the light of day, she could see a bit of Scott in the older gentleman. He had that same colour hair and eyes that Scott did, but his hair was on the lighter side. The woman, however, was just as friendly as her son, she could see where Scott got his charm from. They also possessed the same facial features and dark curly hair. They were a handsome couple indeed.

"Good morn' sunshine. I hope you had a great sleep." Scott's father offered in a boisterous southern voice, that sounded as though it could wake the dead.

"Yes I did, thank you, Sir." She answered politely, still standing in the hall. Not knowing what to do, Piper waited for them to give her more instructions.

"Now, now, none of that, call me Earl, that's what all my friends call me. Sir makes me feel old."

Piper laughed. Accents aside, he sounded just like her own father. She could not remember the amount of times he had said the exact same thing to her friends over the years. She guessed it was the same everywhere you went. Older men really did not like being called sir, it hurt their pride.

"I bet you are famished, look how skinny you are, let's get you fed. Now that you have done the bed part, it's time for the breakfast part." Scott's mother said, as she moved away from them to the Kitchen. Earl escorted her from the hall and held out her chair for her to sit down. Piper took the dining room in. The maple dining table she was seated at looked like it could sit up to twenty people. The windows on the far side encased the whole wall and allowed the occupants inside to view the rolling hills beyond. They were slightly opened which allowed a slight breeze to waft across the table. A chandelier sat above them and sparkled like a hundred jewels. Piper smiled as Scotts mother moved from the kitchen to the dining room, piling the table full of delectable breakfast treats.

Piper's stomach growled as the food kept coming. There was bacon, eggs, scones – or what Americans called biscuits – beans and a wide range of other food. Her eyes settled on a bowl of buttery looking porridge. Piper briefly wondered what it was, and decided that she didn't care, she would try it anyway. Finally, his mother stopped and stood next to the table.

Piper smiled at her motherly instincts, feeling at ease and being reminded of home and her own mother.

"Thank you both. That sounds wonderful, I'm starving and I'm really looking forward to eating some real Alabama food." She smiled warmly, suddenly feeling famished.

"Alrighty. Now eat up Missy." Scott's mother said as stood next to Earl. "May I get you some sweet, iced tea, Honey, or maybe another beverage perhaps?" She asked once Piper had started piling up her plate.

Piper briefly wondered how many people usually stayed here, as she was the only one at the dining table. She was thankful that it was quiet at the moment because she didn't think she could deal with too many people asking her a million questions every morning.

"Just a normal tea would be great, thank you," Piper replied.

Sweet, iced tea seemed to be the beverage of choice down here, but after a few attempts at trying to like the drink, she had decided it was too much for her. She was either a coffee girl or tea with no sugar kinda girl. Every time she drank the sweet, iced tea, her teeth felt as though they would fall out as the sugary sweetness hit them.

Once the tea was served and everyone had sat down, she finished helping herself to the amazing meal. She was pleased to see it was Alabamian food.

The first thing she put on her plate was the porridge looking stuff, which she learnt was grits. She was finally going to try it.

After taking a mouthful though, she was glad she hadn't ordered it at the bar. It was nothing like porridge! The only way Piper could describe it was like eating sand mixed with a shit load of butter. The name suited the meal perfectly, it reminded her of eating gritty sand.

Piper thought about how she could get away with leaving it on her plate *without* offending anyone. She really wanted to spit out the mouthful that she had, but she knew that was beyond bad manners. Doing the only thing she could Piper grabbed her cup of tea, trying to wash the sandy feeling out of her mouth, while she thought up a plan.

"Not a fan." Earl observed as he smiled and winked at her from across the table.

Piper almost chocked on her tea, as she tried to come up with a polite answer.

"No...It's just... I mean..." Piper didn't know what to say. How could she politely tell them that this was disgusting?

Both Mrs. Paisley and Mr. Paisley burst out laughing. "It's alright gal, it's an acquired taste is all. Never you mind about eating the rest." Mr. Paisley offered between chuckles.

Piper breathed in a sigh of relief. The last thing she wanted to do was offend these wonderful people.

"So what's on the agenda today?" Mrs. Paisley asked, as she watched Piper scrape the rest of the grits to the side of her plate. She had just popped a piece of bacon in her mouth in the hopes that the greasy flavour would help, where the tea hadn't.

Piper quickly finished her mouth full of food before she answered. "I'm not sure. I was thinking about maybe checking out the town centre, or maybe even just taking a walk around the farm." Piper thought this would be the perfect time to ask if she could stay longer. She had made the final decision this morning to extend her stay. She just hoped that the couple would have room for her.

"It's a beautiful place you've got here and I'm in no hurry to leave. Would you mind if I booked in for a couple of weeks?" Piper held her breath as she waited for an answer.

Piper let out the breath she had been holding when they both beamed at her. "That would be fantastic, we would love you to stay."

"Who's staying?" came a voice from the stairs.

Piper turned around in her chair at the sound of the new voice. Her eyes widened, and she was dismayed to see the young man that had first hit on her at the bar last night. She closed her eyes groaning, *Why me?*

Piper briefly wondered if the man was also a guest, but that made no sense. Scott had been with this man and his group of friends. The young man whom she guessed was about Jayne's age, ran his hand through is brown hair, it was then that Piper noticed the resemblance to Earl. How was it possible that Piper had offended not one, but two of the Paisley's children. Piper's only hope was that the man had been too drunk to remember anything from last night.

"Oh no way! It's the chick from the bar last night." He said with a smirk, making Piper's blush rise higher. All Piper could hope for now was that he wouldn't let his parents know how rude she had been.

"I hope you're in a better mood this morning." He joked, sitting down and grabbing some breakfast.

Piper was just about to apologise to Hunter, for the way that she had behaved. After the drive home with Scott and a restful night sleep Piper realised that she'd had no right to take her bad mood out on this man. After all he was just doing what any other red blooded male would do. But before she could say anything Mr. Paisley piped up.

"Hunter, please tell me you didn't tell this young lady some of your wise-cracking jokes. What have we told you about scaring off new people?"

Hunter laughed. "Not at all, Pops. All I did was try and ask her out on a date. But never fear she cut me out cold."

Piper turned her eyes to Mr. Paisley, then back to Hunter. Damn, she had managed to insult both of his sons in one day. Hunter winked at her humorously and she sensed a kindness in his eyes that hinted that he wasn't offended in the slightest. She just hoped the father would feel the same. Some people did not take well to their children being insulted.

"Well looks like the gal has got some brains then, doesn't it?" Mr. Paisley laughed, as he got up, slapping his son on the back. Piper noticed that Mr. Paisley had lost his formal demeanour once his son had entered, and the bantering had started.

Looking from Hunter to his father, she realised that he was waiting for her to acknowledge what he said. Piper gave him a slight smile and a nod before she continued eating. After the initial tension of the meeting between her and Hunter, breakfast was actually fun. She laughed at the jokes that the father and son were throwing at each other, and the way they played off each other. The way in which this family interacted reminded her of her own family, in fact in some ways Hunter was similar to Jayne. He was quick witted and smart mouthed. She wouldn't mind betting that he was the outgoing one of the two sons. Sitting with the family made Piper homesick for her own family. It was the first time in days that she felt like she wanted to go home. But she knew that the feeling would pass. It was too soon to go home yet. She still had yet to make a plan. Piper turned her attention back to the family before her dark emotions crept back in. She would not let Cameron spoil this time for her.

Mrs. Paisley acted as though this was a common occurrence, she would shake her head occasionally, but continued eating breakfast and asking Piper general questions about her life. Thankfully she didn't delve too deep and there weren't too many questions about kangaroos. She seemed happy with the simple answers Piper was offering and allowed her privacy without too much probing.

Piper could now see the resemblance between Hunter and Scott; she didn't know why she didn't pick it up last night, though admittedly, she wasn't taking that much notice. She had barely even acknowledged Hunter at all. After breakfast, Piper offered to help clean up, but the Paisleys wouldn't hear of it, so with nothing else to do she decided to go for walk over the property and see what she could find.

<hr>

PIPER HAD BEEN WANDERING over the property for about two hours, when she came across a small private clearing in the creek. It was beautiful, the water appeared to be not too deep, but deep enough in spots to go swimming. It flowed and ebbed along, uninterrupted in its journey. Lush green grass as thick as a carpet made its way to the edge where the small bank dropped off into the creek. It looked as though a seat had been made just for her. It was just what the doctor ordered.

Piper sat down on the edge of the ledge, watching the water rippling along over and around the rocks and trees. It was warm enough that she wished she'd bought her swimmers, but alas they were still packed in her suitcase. She would have to remember to put them on underneath her clothes tomorrow. Thankfully she had taken them on her last dig, otherwise she would have found herself out buying some new ones.

As she sat there, an idea came to her. Suddenly feeling brash and daring Piper looked around to see if there was anybody nearby. She had not come across another soul during her entire trek across the farm, and thankfully she was still alone.

It was perfect.

Pulling her shorts up little bit higher, Piper lowered herself off the ledge and walked into the creek until it reached her knees.

The water was beautiful and she waded around for a bit, keeping an eye out for any pretty thing she could take home. It was something she loved doing. It had started on her first dig out of university, she had found a beautiful shell on one of the islands of Greece and once she made sure she could get it through customs, her tradition had started.

Reaching down, she picked up a smooth rock, but it was not quite what she was looking for. She was just about to drop it when another thought crossed her mind. Skimming it across the water, as she'd done when she was a kid, she was pleased to see she still had the gift.

Piper repeated the action with multiple rocks until she had the rocks skipping five times in a row. Picking up one last rock, she sent it skimming across the creek, six times. Piper was so happy she started hollering and jumping around, she had never been able to skip a rock six times. She had completely forgotten about her shorts and the water had soaked into them, making them practically see through. But she didn't care, she was too free and happy to care about anything at the moment.

That was until the sound of clapping brought her out of her celebration. She turned around to see Scott standing on the bank watching her. He was dressed in a similar way to the way he had been yesterday, only this time the black shirt he wore, was tighter and showed off his muscles to the max. She could also see more of his tattoo today, and she instantly felt her insides clench with lust. Her body screamed for him to take her and take away the pain that she had been feeling. She just wanted to feel something other than doubt, anger and pain. A blush rose over her cheeks, she hoped that he couldn't read her mind. But most of all Piper couldn't believe that she'd been caught acting as though she was a teenager.

"Don't stop on my account. You're doing great," he winked.

Piper offered him a slight smile of embarrassment. Her peace had been broken and she wasn't sure how she felt about it.

"No, it's all good. I'm finished now." Piper added as she quickly waded to the edge of the creek and pulled herself up on to the grassed area beside him.

"Ya know, I've never seen someone do it six times in a row. You must do this all the time."

Piper was grateful that he wasn't going to comment on her wet clothes or appearance. She was starting to make it a habit of meeting him when she was wet.

"It was a fluke, I promise you." She added. At his surprised look Piper added. "I'm serious, I haven't done this since I was a kid. But I must admit, it felt great." Piper knew she should head back to the B&B, she was not sure that she trusted herself to be alone with Scott. But she wasn't ready to lose the peace she had found, even if someone *had* invaded it.

Piper sat down on the grass, hoping that he would leave and yet stay at the same time. She didn't know what it was about this guy, but he made her want something that she just couldn't give at the moment, a part of herself. She was angry at the male population, in her mind they were all just as bad as each other. Yet at the same time, this guy took away some of that anger. She knew it was irrational to hate them all, Piper knew that she couldn't blame them all just because one was a toad. But even though her head told her that, her heart was having trouble letting go of the anger.

If Piper was truthful with herself she knew that the reason her heart felt like that was because she wasn't ready to let go of all the anger just yet; she didn't want to get hurt again or hurt someone else in the meantime. Piper was so confused.

*Why couldn't she just stay angry with everyone? Why did this guy have make her want things she wasn't ready to explore?*

Then a lightbulb moment hit her.

*Was her growing attraction towards Scott her heart's way of getting back at Cameron? Maybe that was it, maybe by sleeping with this guy, she could get all of the anger out of her system, kind of like a rebound. Would that help her move on though?*

Scott would have to know that it would be a short-term thing, she'd already made that clear.

Looking over at Scott, she smiled at his relaxed pose. She was also grateful for it as it gave Piper the chance to study him without him knowing it. She marvelled at the way his arms flexed as he leaned back on them, and the way his heartbeat in his neck was he bathed his face in the sun with this eyes shut. It was then she realised it wouldn't be the worst thing in the world, maybe she could kill two birds with one stone. By sleeping with him she could get her confidence back. Cameron had made her feel worthless and unlovable in that one moment that her world came crashing down. And on the other hand she could get back at Cameron.

But as she continued to watch him doubt invaded her mind. Could she really go through with it? She had never been the type of person that could have a one night stand. She had been with her high school sweetheart for most of her life. How would she even go about it?

*Come on, Pipes, it's just sex,* she heard her sister's voice in her head. As she studied Scott's profile she realised that she was a little excited about the prospect. She was not after anything permanent, been there done that and look where that had gotten her, but a fling sounded nice. The only thing left to do was to figure out how she was going to approach him about it! It wasn't like she could just come out and ask him if he wanted to get jiggy with her. No, she had to work her way into it. Especially after her little speech yesterday about not wanting any kind of relationship.

Remembering that he'd asked her out yesterday, she decided that she would use that as her way in. "Is your offer of showing me around still open?" She spoke, breaking the silence between them.

Scott opened his eyes and turned his head towards her, a small smile forming on his lips – a smile that did all sorts of things to her insides.

"For you darlin'? Anything."

Piper let out a breath she didn't know she had been holding. For some reason she had expected him to renege, but now that she knew he was good for his word, a small part of the weight she had been carrying around lifted off.

"Come on, I challenge you to a rock skimming contest," he said standing up, grabbing her hand and pulling her with him back into the water.

Piper laughed at the playfulness she saw enter his eyes. She wanted nothing more than to let go of everything that was holding her back, and right now was the perfect time to begin.

"Okay, but if I win, you're buying me drinks tonight." Piper waged.

Scott raised an eyebrow at her daring, before adding. "It's a deal, darlin'."

They both walked down to the creek looking for their weapon of choice, and before long the competition was on, but Piper had a feeling that if she did win, she would be winning more than just drinks. She would be winning the experience of a lifetime.

Something she needed right now.

# CHAPTER EIGHT

That night, Piper met Scott at his parents' place. She had offered to meet him somewhere else, but he'd insisted that he'd come and pick her up. His excuse was that it would be less likely for her to get lost if she was with him.

Piper smiled when he drove her to the same bar she'd first met him.

"Our first meeting leave you *that* warm and fuzzy, did it?" Piper asked jokingly.

Scott laughed. "Not at all, darlin', I just brought you back here so you could apologise to the locals for being such a..."

"Hey, watch it, buster." Piper said, hitting his arm as they walked through the door. Piper's heart skipped a beat at the easiness she was feeling with Scott. The afternoon she had spent with him had put her at ease, so much so that she forgot that she was meant to be keeping her distance. Piper glanced over at him to see if her actions had bothered him, but thankfully he played it off as though it hadn't even happened. It was one of the things she was coming to admire about the man. He had a way of making people feel comfortable in any situation.

Piper was amazed at the change in the bar, it was completely different from the other day. Gone was the quite jukebox playing in the corner, as were the families that had been in enjoying a lunchtime meal.

There as still people were everywhere, much like there was the other day, but instead of the lunch time chatter and chaos, loud rambunctious laughter and drunkard conversations filled the bar. Along with the live country band that played against the wall, the bar was full of people country dancing until their heart was content. The quiet lunchtime hang had turned into a downright honkytonk party and Piper loved it.

As Piper looked around, she was relieved to see that she didn't immediately recognise anyone from Scott's table the other day, she would have to do some more apologising if she had, and tonight she didn't want to apologise to anyone, she simply wanted to let loose and forget about everything in her life, everything but tonight.

Scott put his hand in the middle of her back and walked her to the bar where they ordered some drinks. She pulled her wallet out to pay, as she had lost the rock skimming contest after all, but before she could Scott shook his head.

"My aunty owns the bar, I will talk to her about you starting a tab." Piper opened her mouth to argue, but he stopped her.

"Look darlin', it's the way it is done down here." He said before she could get a word out.

Piper simply smiled and put her wallet away. There was no use arguing with him, she would just come in here tomorrow and square it away, she didn't want anything that would tie her here if she had to leave in a hurry. Piper's heart twinged a little at the thought of leaving, but no sooner had it came it was gone.

It wasn't long before his aunty came over and introduced herself. She was a slender woman with the same jet-black hair that Scott possessed, she guessed for her looks that she was Scott's mother's sister. And just like her sister and nephew, she was warm and welcoming. Piper knew that she was going to have a hard time not liking the woman.

Five minutes later, his aunt headed back to work, but not before introducing her to Susie, the bartender that would look after them for the night.

Scott excused himself to go to the bathroom, while Piper ordered their drink from Susie. Susie was young, about Piper's age, but she had none of Piper's bitterness. She guessed that the world had yet to kick Susie where it hurt. For a split second Piper felt envy towards the young woman, but the moment Susie smiled warmly at Piper all of the envy vanished. Piper hoped that the woman never lost her love for life, that Susie never had to feel the pain Piper felt.

"What will you have, ma'am," Susie asked in her Southern accent.

"Jack and Coke, please," Piper answered, loving the way she had been called ma'am. It was a hidden pleasure of hers. Ever since she'd heard it said on her favourite show, Piper had secretly hoped that one day a Southern man would call her that while making love. She had never dreamed it would come to pass of course, but now that she was here, and single, maybe something else could be ticked off of her fantasy list.

As Susie poured her drink, she asked Piper about herself, brining Piper out of her daydream. Piper gave her the usual spiel before asking Susie the same questions. Piper was surprised that, as she talked with the young woman, she started to feel herself relax. There was no malice in Susie, just open, honest friendship. Something she was only just now starting to realise had truly been missing from her and Karen's relationship. Piper wondered briefly when it had disappeared.

As they stood there talking, Piper learnt that Susie had just moved here herself a little over a month ago. She was just about to ask her what she thought of the town, when Scott was behind her.

"Come on, darlin', I want to introduce you to some people."

Piper would have preferred to stay and talk to Susie, but once he had their drinks Scott led her over to a table full of more of his friends, none of whom had been there the day before. He introduced her and immediately they welcomed her into their fold.

At first Piper had been quiet and only answered when the questions came her way, but as the night went on, Piper began to relax and was surprised to find that she was having a ball. It wasn't long before Piper found herself having a lively discussion about the benefits of living in America over Australia.

"You have all types of animals that want to kill you." He argued.

"You have bears." She quipped back.

"You have droughts."

"You have earthquakes and tornados"

"You have long highways with nothing in-between"

Piper laughed at that one. "So do you."

The guy laughed and took another sip of his drink, she could see him thinking of another one, but before he could get it out Scott grabbed her attention,

"Hey, you wanna dance?" he asked her out of the blue.

Piper looked out at the dance floor, as an upbeat song played out a danceable rhythm that wouldn't mean close contact. This would mean that she could dance and have fun without having to touch him just yet. She would have to get more intimate with him later, but she wanted to build up to it. Dancing would allow her to do this as she could start out with your general dancing, but it would allow her to chuck in some of her signature moves. She knew she was a good dancer as she had been doing it since she was a kid.

"Sure, let's go," she said, making the decision. She grabbed his hand and pulled him onto the dance floor.

The song finished just as they hit the dance floor and a new song started, Piper was excited to see that it was a line dance. She hadn't done line dancing since she was at school, but she'd loved doing it.

"Do you want to sit down?" Scott asked.

She laughed and shook her head. "No way, buddy, let's get our country on."

Scott looked at her curiously as they lined up. "You ready, darlin?" He winked at her when she nodded.

"As ready as I'll ever be," Piper laughed,

"Don't worry, darlin', if it gets too hard, just follow me."

Piper danced alongside him, laughing as he missed a few steps and then laughing harder when she missed more. It was a great night, but before long, it was over.

Piper had a little bit more to drink than she remembered, and she was feeling happier than she had in weeks. This place was just what she needed, she needed a quiet farm where she could roam free, and she needed a night out which involved fun and drinking, a night that took her mind off what had happened.

As she got in Scott's truck, her phone buzzed with a special tone, alerting her that it was from her sister. Her mood sobering, she opened the text.

Sis: *Hey Pipes just letting U know that Cameron was here 2day he got a little bit huffy demanding that we tell him where U were. But don't worry I told him that U had not contacted us yet. That was when he lost his goddam mind, he started blowing up, screaming at me that this was bullshit. Mum and Dad handled it, but I didn't let him get away completely unscathed. No Siree, I let him know in my own way that I knew what was going on. After that he left with his tail between his legs. Mum and Dad are good they think UR on a holiday. Keep safe and don't forget to let me know how UR going! TTFN*

Piper stared at the message, her anger on the rise again. *Why couldn't he just let her go? He knew that he had made a massive mistake. Why did he have to bring her family into it for Christ's sake? He was the one that had cheated on her and he was acting like she'd done him wrong.*

So much for all of the cheering up she'd done tonight. It had just been thrown out the window, Piper was pissed and she wanted to punch someone, well she knew exactly who she wanted to punch but he wasn't here.

Scott climbed into the other side of the truck and took one look at her face. The moment his brows furrowed and concern entered his eyes she knew what he was seeing. He was seeing the same Piper he had seen the first day they had meet, and she didn't want that. She didn't want to ruin their night. She hoped that he would let it go, but no such luck.

"What's up, darlin', my dancing wasn't that bad." He joked lightly, but Piper only gave a have hearted laugh. It was all she could muster.

Piper knew that he was trying to break the somber pall that had come over her, but it just wasn't working. "I just need to go back to the B&B. I think I drunk too much and I need to go to sleep that's all.

I have a bit of a headache." She let out the breath she had been holding when he didn't pry any deeper. She knew from the tenseness in his shoulder, and the continued frown on his face that he didn't buy her story. Thankfully though he didn't pry any deeper. Piper felt a little guilty for ruining their night, but she couldn't stop the pain that was entering her heart once more.

"Okay, but if there's anything I can do to help, just let me know." He whispered quietly before he put the truck in gear and started to drive down the road.

Piper looked over at him, trying to block out the images of Cameron and Karen that hammered on inside of her mind. As they barraged her Scott's words hit her, and she knew of one way that he *could* make her feel better. Piper knew she'd probably regret it in the morning, but right now she didn't care. She just wanted, no *needed*, to feel like she was beautiful again, like she was loveable. To feel like she was desirable, and she knew this man could make that happen.

"I'll let you know." She said not revealing any of her thoughts. Piper decided she would use the ride home to make her final decision, it wasn't like she could attack him here in the car while they drove down the road. She should at least wait until they got home and, if she still felt the same way when they got there, then she'd make her move. And if he decided that he was interested in what she was offering, then she made a promise to herself that she wasn't gonna hold back, she was gonna enjoy her one-night stand with everything she had.

Maybe, if it was good, and she decided to stay, she might give it another go, but for now one night was what she was aiming for. Maybe a one night stand was exactly what she needed to mend her heart and get Cameron out of it for good.

# CHAPTER NINE

Scott didn't know what was going on in the beauty's head. They'd had a great night, he knew it. He loved watching her drink and dance and do all the fun things that he loved doing and he could almost swear that she was actually starting to dig him. As the night wore on he could see her icy exterior slowly start to melt away with each smile she gave him. But by the time he had closed her door and walked around to open his, her happiness had left, her icy exterior was back, and she now had a cloud hanging over her, the same cloud that had been there when he had first met her.

When she looked at him, the same anger and irritation that he had seen in them the day they met was back. He knew he hadn't done anything wrong, and he wanted nothing more than to know what had put that sadness there. But Scott could tell from her demeanour that she didn't want to talk about it and he didn't want to dredge up anything more that would add to her misery. The drive home was silent, it was nothing like the ride to the bar, during the trip in Piper had been talkative and asked a million questions about the town he lived in, now she simply sat quietly and looked out the window at the darkness outside. A darkness he sensed she felt inside.

Scott looked over and saw her checking her phone multiple times and every time she did her mood darkened.

"Do you want to talk? My momma says a burden shared, is a load lightened." He tried once more.

He saw a small smile soften her lips. But still she stayed clammed up. He gave up trying and respected her wishes. He caught her looking at him a couple of times, and while he knew she didn't want to talk about what was bothering her, he couldn't take the silence anymore. He decided to ask her a safe question, well it should have been safe.

"So you never did tell me what brought you to our slice of heaven."

"Trust me it's the same old story, one that you don't want to hear." She said, bitterness lacing her voice.

"Come on, it can't be all *that* bad," he joked.

"Does walking in on your fiancé screwing your best friend, a *friend*, mind you, that had been your best friend since primary school, count as bad in your book? If not, what does?" Piper spat.

Scott knew the moment the words left her mouth that she hadn't meant to say them as her face went white, as if realising that she'd said too much. She hung her head and went back to looking out the window.

*So that was it.*

Scott instantly understood and his heart went out to her. "Well yeah that is bad, but I say his loss is my gain. If he was stupid enough to let you go then he didn't deserve you." Scott looked at her when she faced him again, he saw surprise in her eyes and her body straightened a bit as though she didn't believe him. Her eyes shone bright in the dim light of the moon as through she was trying to hold back tears. It broke his heart to see her in such pain, he could have killed the guy that made her question her worth.

"Come on darling, you have to know what you look like, you can make any man turn to sin." He added with a shrug, he was not going to apologies for telling the truth.

Her eyes were glued to him. He wanted her to say something, but he was not going to push her. When she didn't say anything more and just sat silently in her seat looking back out the window, he wondered if he had gone too far.

*Nice one Scott, creep the girl out why don't you.*

He wondered where all of his charm had gone. It had seemed to disappear the moment this woman entered his life.

Moments later they were pulling up into the yard of the B&B. Scott put the truck in park, got out, walked around to her side and opened the door. His father had always taught him to open doors for the women that entered his life, down south it was breed into boys at a young age to be gentlemen. "Everyone deserved to feel special," he would say, and Scott knew that tonight Piper needed that more than ever.

They walked to the door quietly, and before he could stop himself, he lent down and kissed her goodnight.

Piper looked at him, her eye as wide a saucers, and before she could say anything, he added, "look, I'm sorry. I know you probably didn't want that, but I just wanted to let you know that I had a great time and I wanted to thank you properly. Don't read anything into it."

Scott waited for her to say something, but when she simply licked her lips he turned on his heel and stared to walk off. He hadn't gone three steps down the porch however, when he thought better off it.

Turning around to face her again he spoke his mind. "Piper, some people are just jerks, okay. They don't deserve to have people like you in their lives and you shouldn't let them drag you down to their level." When she didn't respond, he turned again and started to leave, but he let out a breath when her hand reached out, stopping him.

Scott was shocked when she walked around him, and without a word, planted her lips on his. That was all the invitation he needed. He picked her up and she wrapped her legs around him. Turning back towards his parents' place, he paused as he thought better of taking her there. It had been year since he had slept with a woman in his parents place, and the last encounter had left him scared.

He could still see his mother's look as though it had happened yesterday, when she walked in on him and his date buck naked halfway through intercourse. He had promised himself from that day forward he would never sleep with a woman in his parents' house again.

Scott had to think of something quick. He wasn't sure he could hold any longer with the way that Piper was kissing his neck and biting at his ears. Damn the woman was hot. Looking around Scott tried to think of an alternative plan, the minute his eyes landed on the barn he knew he had it. Making sure that Piper's legs were wrapped tightly around his waist, Scott made his way to the barn out the back. Once there he opened the door and walked her over to the pile of hay, covered with a tarp.

His heart was pounding in his chest, and he knew that no matter what he was not going to let Piper leave tonight without her knowing how amazing she was.

Tonight was not about him, tonight was all about her. He would make it a night for her to remember if it was the last thing he did.

# CHAPTER TEN

*P*iper loved how he carried her; the way her legs wrapped around his waist so that his manhood met her core, and the way his hands rested on her arse, holding her tight to him. It was as though she weighed nothing.

Right now Scott was kissing her all over, as though he wanted to devour her. When his tongue slipped in and mingled with hers the waves of passion hit her all the way to core. *This* was what she needed.

Piper noted briefly that she was laying on hay, but she didn't care. She had already decided that she wanted this any way she could get it, and the moment he kissed her and said those words, he had sealed their fate.

In a frenzy of arms and legs, they stripped each other down. He pulled out a condom from his pants pocket and before she knew what was happening, he was inside of her; no foreplay was needed. Piper was already wet from the way he had been kissing her, and from the way her center had rubbed along his cock as they'd walked to the barn. All night she had been thinking of nothing more than getting this guy into bed.

Piper moaned as he rode her hard. Scott was so thick that her entire core felt as though she was full. She could feel the tip of his manhood hit her womb when he pounded inside of her once more. The rhythm was neither too slow, nor too fast, it was just enough to keep Piper on the brink of coming, without actually driving her over the edge. Never before had the sex with Cameron been this good. With him Cameron always reached the brink of ecstasy before she did, and sometimes Piper even found herself finishing herself off later. She had never questioned this before, because she loved Cameron.

Her mind was swiftly brought back to reality when Scott started driving his cock in and out of her harder, it was fast at first and then slow. The pulsating movements he was using caused her insides to quiver, building with tension once more.

All thoughts of her ex left her mind as she focused on what Scott was doing to her. The more he moved, the more the pain and anger from the past few weeks faded away. All she felt now was passion so raw that it left her burning for more.

A few days ago she didn't think she could ever feel this way again. Piper was about to lose her mind, she didn't know how much more of this bliss she could take. Her heart raced, and she could feel the pulse in her neck beating in time with it.

Every nerve was pulled so taught that any slight change in his rhythm could snap them. Piper moaned as she felt his stomach muscles tense, indicating that he too was on the brink. Her back arched as she moaned and, just when she didn't think she could take any more, he put his hand down between them and massaged her clit. That was her undoing.

In an avalanche of overwhelmingly intense feelings, Piper cascaded over the edge, screaming his name as her whole body filled with the fireworks that was her orgasm. Piper felt him tense once more as he reached his own peak. There was no scream from him, just a long moan that Piper felt throughout her body, sending her spiralling back over the edge of bliss.

When the last pulse of her orgasm faded Piper sighed, she'd never dreamt it would be this good, and there hadn't even been any foreplay. Piper knew that she would be feeling the aftermath of their love making for days.

Once they were both sated, Scott collapsed his weight on her which she didn't mind. Piper felt his breath even out and she wondered briefly if he had fallen asleep.

"Damn darlin' you're gonna kill me if you keep that up."

Piper chuckled, she hadn't realised that she had been rubbing her hands idly along his body as he lay there, content. Piper stopped moving her hands along his body. With that, he rolled off her and then stood up. Piper immediately felt the cool night air and she wanted nothing more than to grab him and pull him back to her.

"Come with me," he said, holding out his hand. Piper didn't give it a second thought. Grabbing his hand she followed him into a tiny bathroom that had been attached to the barn. He turned the water on and Piper raised her eyebrows at him.

"You didn't think it was gonna end there did you darlin'?"

Piper looked at him in surprise.

"Come on, *that* was just the start, into the shower with you, where we can continue."

Piper giggled and did what he asked. She did promise herself one night after all and the night was far from finished.

Piper was glad she hadn't let it end there as Scott was true to his word, they didn't leave the barn till the early hours of the morning when he snuck her back into the house before kissing her goodbye and leaving.

As she stared at the ceiling in the comfort of her bed, part of her felt as though she should feel ashamed, but she didn't. With that realisation came another, Piper decided that if Scott wanted to continue fooling around while she was here, she wouldn't be opposed to it. Piper just had to make sure that she didn't get attached. She would make sure Scott knew that before they went any further. She drifted into a sleep that was no longer filled with betrayal, but of a sexy Alabamian man who made her world seem whole, if only for a short time.

---

PIPER WOKE the next morning with a huge smile on her face. Her body still ached from the fun that she and Scott had had the night before. Turning on her side, Piper laid her head into her pillow, she swore she could still smell his aftershave. Piper shook her head at her fancy, she needed to stop thinking like that. If this was going to work she needed to remember that it was only going to be physical.

Moments later her heart betrayed her when she heard the rev of his truck come down the driveway. She wondered if he was as excited as she was to see him. She knew she needed to have the conversation with him, but for now she would be happy just seeing his smiling face.

Piper quickly jumped out of bed and sprung into the shower. It was one of the quickest showers she'd had in a while. It didn't help the fact that as she soaped herself, Piper was flooded with memories of Scott doing the same thing to her last night. Turning the water off, and putting all memories of last night out of her mind, Piper quickly dried her hair and got dressed.

She was practically running down the stairs when she heard Scott with his parents and brother in the dining room. When she reached the bottom of the stairs, Piper took a quick minute to steady her breathing and get her heartbeat under control. She knew it was silly to think that anyone would know anything had happened, but Piper still wanted to make sure.

When she felt as though she was ready she causally strode into the dining room, and took her normal seat. She smiled to see that a nice cup of tea was already waiting for her.

"Good morning everyone." She answered, smiling at Scotts parents and Hunter. She had yet to meet Scott's eyes as she was not sure what her reaction would be.

"Morning, how are we this fine morning." Earl asked her.

Piper took a sip of her drink before answering. "Fine thank you." She answered. Piper knew she was sounding too formal, but she couldn't help it. Hunter narrowed his eyes on her and she wondered if he knew something. Surly not. Piper was pretty sure that Scott would not have shared what happened between them with his brother.

"I take it Scott showed you a good time last night." Their mother asked, unbeknownst to the turmoil that was going through Piper's mind.

She almost choked on her tea, when she asked that question, and Piper had no choice but to look at Scott when he replied.

"Would you expect anything else Ma. But rest assured I was a *complete* gentleman."

Piper looked at Scott and was just in time to catch him wink at her. She knew there was an underlying meaning to his words, but thankfully no-one else understood.

"That's nice dear." His mother replied, and soon everyone was talking about their plans for the day and Piper was able to settle in and eat, while laughing with the family, today was going to be a good day she knew it.

---

"Care to take a walk with me?" Scott asked from just behind Piper. As she turned to look at him, it took all of her will power not to lean forward and kiss him. She sure did want to take a walk with him, as she wanted to get their conversation out of the road so that they could start their fling, or whatever it would be.

"That would be lovely," Piper answered.

As they walked out of the house and into the morning sun, Piper's nerves began to take over. She didn't know how Scott was going to take her proposal. What if it offended him somehow? Even worse what if he didn't like last night as much as she had. Doubt after doubt started to fill Piper's mind and she was afraid that if she didn't get her words out soon she was going to chicken out.

"Piper."

"Scott."

They said at the same time. Both looked at each other and started to laugh. "It is good to see I am not the only one who is nervous." Scott joked as he opened the barn door for her to enter. As she looked around in the light of day, memories of what they had done last night once again flooded her senses and she knew that she had to ask him. The last thing Piper wanted was for last night to be the final time she got to sleep with Scott.

"I have a proposition for you." Piper blurted out before she lost her nerve.

She looked at Scott to gauge his reaction. Piper had to smile as she saw him sitting on the hay bales, leaning back on his hands the way he had at the river. She was starting to learn that he did that when he was trying to put her at ease.

"A proposition hey." He asked raising his eyebrows.

"Yes, a proposition. But before I tell you what it is you must promise to let me get through the whole of it before you make your decision."

Piper waited to see what he would say, she watched as he pondered her request. She wasn't entirely sure if he did it for his own benefit or if he was just making fun of her, either way she didn't care, she only cared that he agreed.

"You got it ma'am."

And there it was. Those words she had longed to hear. Piper had to close her eyes, and ball her fists at her side to stop herself from begging him to take her again.

"Piper?"

At the sound of his name coming from his lips, Piper opened her eyes to see that his cool relaxed demeanour was gone. His eyes no longer held the laughter they had earlier, instead they were now full of the same lust that had been present the evening before.

"I think it is time that you state your proposition darlin'" Scott whispered as he got down from the hay bale and stood in front of her.

His body was so close that she could feel the heat coming from it. Of its own accord Piper's hand glided up and rested on his chest.

"Well you see, I thought that we could..... well..." Piper seemed to be having trouble getting her words out. Scott's hand had come to rest on her neck and she could not stop herself from leaning into his touch. Goosebumps rose all of her skin, when he ran his thumb along her lips, and Piper couldn't resist tasting him.

"We could, what?" Scott asked in a husky voice. Piper looked up at him with hooded eyes. She was glad she was not the only one effected by the other's nearness. She had to shake her head to clear her thoughts. She knew she had something important to discuss, but right now she was having trouble remembering what that was.

"Your proposition." Scott prompted bring his lips close to her ear.

Piper gave in and leaned against him. Yes her proposition. She needed to get his agreement and fast so that they could get down to more enjoyable things.

"Well, I thought that we could continue doing what we did last night, for as long as I am here."

"Mmmm, I like the sound of that." Scott murmured, as he kissed her neck. Piper loved what he was doing and she loathed the thought of him stopping. But she needed to make sure that he understood everything.

"There is one stipulation." Piper added.

That sentence cooled Scott's lust pretty quick. She was not sure exactly what was going through his mind.

"And that would be?" he asked in a tight tone.

Piper lowered her gaze as she said the next words. "You have to promise me that there will be no strings attached. We both have to understand that this is merely for fun, nothing will come for it."

The silence that rang down on here was deafening, she wasn't sure if she had insulted him or not, but she needed him to know where she stood. Piper was in no shape to start something with someone else. Her heart was still mending and it was not fair to Scott to promise him anything else.

As the silence continued, Piper finally go the nerve to look up at him. There was no anger, or pity, only understanding.

"This is what you want?" Scott asked with a sweet smile.

Piper nodded her head, "then so be it." He answered. Piper knew that she should have felt relief, instead she felt as though she was missing out on something. The feeling didn't last however, because no sooner had he said the words, Scott picked her up and carried her to the place they had made love last night.

"I guess we should make it official then shouldn't we." He stated, right before he kissed her.

Any other arguments that she might have formed left her mind the moment his lips met hers, and it wasn't unit much later that night that Piper realised Scott hadn't given her an actual answer. She knew she should be mad, but Piper couldn't bring herself to feel that way, not after the day they had just spent together.

Piper would just have to watch her own heart, because she would be dammed if she was giving up her affair with Scott. She had a feeling that he was exactly what the doctor ordered, and she was going to have her fill of him if it was the last thing she did.

# CHAPTER ELEVEN

Over the next week, Piper and Scott spent all of their time together, most of the time was spent at his place. They didn't like the idea of his parents finding out what was going on, especially since they were growing fond of her, but the main reason that Piper gave herself was that she knew she would be moving on soon.

As they got to know each other, Piper learnt that Scott was in construction and he loved showing her some of the houses he was working on. She was also delighted to know that he was working on becoming an architect. He explained that he not only loved to build housed, but he also loved to design them. Piper knew from the way he talked about every aspect of a home that Scott had a true passion and understanding of what made a house a home. Piper wasn't surprised in the least when Scott had informed her that he had built and designed his own home. Scott's house was a simple one-story wood cabin, with a wrap-around veranda. It suited his personality to a tee, it was simple, yet elegant, and warm, everything that Scott himself portrayed.

Each piece of wood that Scott had used for the walls had been polished to perfection and placed perfectly, giving it that rustic country look. Floor to ceiling doors opened out on to the patio. Piper would never forget the first time she walked inside, she was in awe of his craftsmanship. Every piece of furniture was made of the same wood that he had used outside, all polished and tinted in differing complementary shades. The fireplace that stood against the far wall of the living room offered an extra country charm. The roof was not flat inside as most rooves were, instead it was completely open, with only rafters running across it for support.

As she looked around the magnificently designed and crafted house, Piper couldn't help but be impressed. For a small-town country boy, he had talent. She ran her hands over the highly polished wood of the dining table, marvelling at its smooth texture. Country boy definitely had skill. Piper smiled to herself as she remembered what other things his skilled hands were good at.

The rest of their time was spent wandering the farm or checking out the State of Alabama. Scott was giving her the guided tour of his state. It often afforded them the chance to stay in a motel overnight, far from prying eyes.

Today they were just down by the river fishing and having a picnic; just lazing about – it was Sunday after all.

Piper looked over at Scott who was laying down on the blanket, while his fishing rod sat perched in the bank. Piper had never liked going fishing before, she never had the patients for it. But today even though they hadn't caught many fish, Piper did not mind. For now she had other things on her mind. Scott being one of them.

He had his arm thrown up over his eyes and his shirt had lifted up, showing her his abs, where another tattoo ran the length of his side. Over the past few weeks Piper had gotten a good look at his many tattoos, she was pleased to note that every single one of them turned her on. Especially the one she was seeing now.

Feeling mischievous, Piper crawled over to him, lifted his shirt and bit his abs, before sliding her tongue up and over the sprawled eagle, carrying the Alabama state flag.

Scott growled. "If you keep that up, darlin, you will have to pay the price."

Piper just smiled at him before nipping him again. She slowly kissed her way down to the waist of his jeans, before she teased his buttons undone and pulled his pants down, allowing his cock to spring free. Piper didn't know what it was about Scott that made her wild, but over the last few weeks she had learnt to let her guard down and follow her inhibitions, and it felt great.

Piper admired his cock for a few minutes, running her nails along the shaft and below to his sack. She was pleased to hear the moans from deep within. Looking up a smile played on her lips as she noticed that his eyes were now shut, but he was anything but relaxed. Feeling bolder than she had in years, Piper took the tip into her mouth, before allowing herself to suck him from the tip to the base and then back up again in slow, drawn out movements. The groan that escaped him rumbled through her. Piper loved the power she had over him, but she also loved the sense she got from being out in the open making love.

Piper continued until she was grabbed by the arms and Scott's lips were smashed to hers – their tongues entwined in a hot passionate kiss.

Unable to hold back her passion any longer Piper straddled him, while keeping their lips connected. She hissed when Scott reached down between them, ripped her panties to the side before sinking two fingers deep inside of her.

Piper reared up, unable to control the pleasure pulsing through her as his fingers worked their magic inside of her, his thumb stroking her clitoris bringing her closer to her peak.

"So wet and tight," she heard him mutter.

Writhing in anticipation Piper moaned as she was brought closer to cascading over the precipice, when he pulled his fingers out.

"Scott," she begged, unable to utter anything else.

"Not without me, darlin'. I want to feel you squeeze me as you cum." His voice was rough with heat.

Piper looked down into his passion-filled eyes, he slid into her until he was embedded to the hilt and they both moaned in unison. Piper began to ride him, slow at first, and when she could no longer take it, she sped up and rode him hard until they both found their release. Sweet dripped from her body as pulse after pulse of ecstasy rushed through her body. They panted heavily under the exertion and Piper fell forward, collapsing against his chest that was where she stayed. With the sun beating down on them and nature everywhere around, Piper felt as though she was in her very own private heaven. A heave she had no desire to leave anytime soon.

"Damn, I swear it gets better each time," Scott said from beneath her.

Piper lifted her hips off him, and moaned again at the feeling of him sliding out. She couldn't get enough of this guy.

"How about we pack up and take this back to your place?" Piper suggested.

"Sounds like a plan, I just need a minute. I'm not sure my legs will carry me at the moment." Scott joked weakly.

Piper laughed as she rolled off him onto her back, to where she now lay on the blanket. She was just about to reply when her phone suddenly chimed. Piper had no desire to answer it, but before she had time decide if she was going to check who had messaged her, it chimed again and again. Something was wrong. Piper knew she had to answer it now. But she had just picked it up when the *Shameless* tone rang through.

"Hey Jayne." she said answering on the third ring, a little surprised and a little irritated that her afternoon fun was being interrupted. But any thoughts of the wonderful afternoon she had imagined left her the moment her sister's tone came through the phone.

"What the hell! Why didn't you answer your messages, I have sent you like three, Goddammit, Pipes!"

"Hang on a minute, before you start yelling at me, the phone messages just came through. I was just about to answer them when you rang."

The urgency in Jayne's did not go unnoticed by Piper. "What's going on? Is Mum and Dad okay?"

"Yes, Mum and Dad are okay, but you gotta listen okay. I just found out that three days ago Cameron figured out where you were."

Piper's heart started beating at a rapid pace and her blood went cold. This wasn't supposed to happen this quickly. She was supposed to have more time. Once again Cameron was going to bring her world was going to come crashing down, only this time she had more to lose.

## CHAPTER TWELVE

"What? How?" Piper's voice had become shrill. When Scott turned to look at her, she realised what she had done. The last thing she needed was for Scott to become worried, all that would lead to is questions, and Piper wasn't sure she had the answers for the questions he was sure to ask.

Piper shook her head letting him know that everything was okay, even though it wasn't. She had no idea how she was going to get out of this one, her mind was working overtime trying to come up with a plan.

"Apparently, you used your joint credit card to pay for the B&B you're staying at and it came up on the statement. But that's not all. I am sorry to tell you this, but Pipes, he got straight on a plane. I didn't find this out until just now, and it was only by chance that I heard Karen talking about it with Mum. Can you believe that bitch has the audacity to come here and act like everything is normal....."

Piper didn't hear the rest of what her sister was talking about, her mind was still on the fact that Cameron was on his way. She would deal with the whole Karen situation another day, all Piper cared about was figuring out how much time she had left to get herself out of here.

"Jayne, how long?"

Her sister paused in her ranting, "how long for what?"

"Until he gets her Jayne, how long?"

Piper felt her hope crumble as Jayne paused. Then the news she had been dreading the most came.

"I heard Karen tell Mum that he was in Alabama. I don't know exactly when he should get to the town you're in, but I would say any time now. I'm sorry, sis, I didn't know. If I'd known sooner I would've let you know." Piper could hear the guilt in her sister's voice, and she felt bad as she knew it wasn't her fault. It was Cameron's fault. He had already broken her heart, why did he feel the need to come and break her peace as well. Why couldn't he just let her go.

Piper's heart beat so fast it hurt. She'd known it had been a bad idea to use her card, but she had been on edge after her drive with Scott, and being wet and tired didn't help, she had simply reverted to her natural instinct. Piper hadn't even realised what she had done until after the fact. She had been praying that Cameron wasn't smart enough to check the account, but as luck would have it he had.

Piper couldn't waste any more time she had to get off the phone as soon as possible so she could get out of dodge.

"It's okay, Jayne, it's not your fault. Thanks for letting me know, look I've gotta go." Piper didn't want to say much more as she knew Scott was listening. She didn't want any arguments from him, so she thought it best to just disappear. That was what she told herself, but she knew the truth. Piper wasn't sure she could say goodbye. Even with all of her best intentions, Piper had become attached. But not just to Scott, to the whole damn family. If Piper was honest with herself she would know that she never wanted to leave this slice of heaven. All she wanted to do was continue living her in her own bubble, enjoying life while her heart mended.

But it was not meant to be.

"Okay, but stay safe and let me know where you end up next."

"I will." With that Piper hung up the phone. There was no goodbye, no I love you, Piper only had one thing on her mind.

Running.

Piper sat where she was, staring at her phone trying to gather her thoughts. She knew she couldn't just jump up and leave as that would look suspicious, besides, Scott was smart enough to put two and two together if she left now. All she could do was continue on with their afternoon long enough until she could feigned a headache.

But it was harder than Piper thought it would be to keep up the happy appearance. All she could think about was how much it was going to hurt to leave here, and what she was going to do now that Cameron was in America. Piper thought she had done a stellar job at keeping her thoughts to herself.

"So are we going to go and finish this up at my place?" Scott asked her about a half an hour after her phone call.

Piper almost slapped her forehead, how could she have forgotten what they had planned. Her body screamed at her to take the opportunity to enjoy his lush body one more time, but her head warned her against it. As much as Piper wanted to listen to her heart, she knew her head was right, she had no idea how long she had, and she could not afford to waste the time she did have.

Leaning into Scott, Piper ran her hand down Scott's still bear chest and kissed his cheek before saying, "that sounds divine, but can you take a rain-check for now, I have a bit of a headache and think I would like to take a nap before our dinner tonight."

Scott pulled her close and kissed her neck, before replying, "I could take a nap with you."

Piper laughed at that and pulled away. She stood up and started moving around collecting all of their stuff. "And we know how that will end, don't we." Piper winked and offered him a smile.

Scott tilted his head and Piper worried that she might have taken the ruse too far. But when he smiled she let out the breath she had been holding. "Alright, but I plan on having you make it up to me later darlin'" Scott added as he stood up and pulled her to him for a passionate kiss.

Piper didn't say anything she simply wrapped her arms around his neck and kissed him back. Piper put everything she had into the kiss. Her heart ached with the knowledge that this would probably be the last time she ever saw this man. Before the tears began to fall Piper pulled away and started packing up once more. She needed to get away from this man before she told him everything.

Once they had packed up their picnic, they headed back towards the B&B. Piper was quiet on the ride home, she was lost in her thoughts, and she didn't know if she could continue lying to Scott. As the B&B came into view Piper started to calm down a little she was almost in the clear. But as they got out of the car and neared the steps, Scott spoke, and Piper knew she hadn't fooled him one little bit.

"What's going on, darlin'?"

Piper stopped on the bottom step and looked at him. She thought about lying to him, but when she looked to his eyes and thought about the happiness he had brought her over the past few weeks she knew he deserved better than that.

"Look, this has been great, but I have to go." Piper felt guilty at the hurt look that came to his eyes. She had expected him to be surprised, but she was not expecting the pain she saw there.

"Why?" Scott walked up the step to stand beside her. Piper took a deep breath and closed her eyes. She didn't want to say the words out loud, because that would make them true.

"Because my ex is on his way here and I am not ready to face him. I cannot be here when he gets here. I need to get out of town." Piper's voice broke as she said the last part. It was killing her knowing that she was going to have to leave this place. She hadn't meant to get attached, but she had.

Piper turned from the pain she saw in his eyes, she didn't want to hear is arguments for why she should stay because Piper wasn't sure that she wouldn't let him talk her into it. Before Scott could say any more, she ran up the stairs. Part of Piper hoped that Scott would follow her inside and beg her not to go but when she heard his car start up and drive down the long drive she knew it was over. Piper threw herself on her bed and cried, she cried for everything she had lost the first time Cameron had ruined her life, and she cried for what she was losing now.

Once the tears had stopped following Piper got to work, she quickly packed her bags, then headed downstairs to say goodbye to the Paisleys. A sad smile played on her lips when she got to the bottom of the staircase and heard them talking with Hunter in the dining room. Earl and Hunter were paying out on each other once more, while Scott's mother talked about what was going on in town. Tears threatened to flow once more as she realised that she was never going to hear this again. Who knew how long it would be before she got back this way.

Mrs. Paisley was the first one to see Piper. She got up from the table and walked around to give her a hug.

"We thought you were out with Scott, otherwise we would have saved you some lunch." She added as she hugged Piper.

Piper hugged the woman back and cherished the feel of her arms around her one last time.

"I was, but I had a bit of a headache so I came home for a lie down." Piper was trying to find the courage to tell them that she was leaving when Earl looked at what she was holding.

"Going somewhere?"

With that comment Hunter and Mrs. Paisley looked down at her feet to where some of her luggage sat. Piper could no longer hold back the tears and simply nodded.

Mr. Paisley got up and walked to her, he embraced Piper in a bear hug.

"Well, we sure are going to miss you around here." He added.

"Does Scott know?" Hunter asked as he too stood up from the table to say his goodbyes.

Piper couldn't say anything as her throat was hurting from the tears she was holding back, so she simply nodded.

"Well it sure is a shame, I was just getting used to you being here." Hunter added as he to embraced her.

When Piper looked over to see tears in Mrs. Paisley's eyes she knew she had to get out of there. It was bad enough walking away from the pain in Scott's eyes, this was only making it ten times worse.

"I want to truly thank you for allowing me to stay here. It was exactly what I needed." Piper offered wiping a tear from her eye as she bent down to get her bags.

"Here let me." Hunter as he grabbed them for her and took them to the car.

The Paisley's walked with her outside to her car, before they all gave her one more hug. "Don't be a stranger." Earl whispered as he hugged her once more.

"Make sure you keep I touch." Mrs. Paisley added, rubbing Piper's arm before she got into her car.

Piper waited until she heard Hunter close her boot before she started the car. When Hunter joined his parents, Piper said her final goodbye and reversed out of the drive.

Looking back in her mirror, the picture of the Paisleys waving to her, tears running down Mrs. Paisley's face tore at her heart. Piper knew that she was never going to find a place like this again, and as the tears feel freely now she once again cursed Cameron for running her life.

Only this time Piper didn't want to run, she wanted more than anything to stay.

But it was not to be. Piper put her blinker on to turn on to the main road and began the next leg of her journey. A journey she was no longer excited to be on.

## CHAPTER THIRTEEN

iper had almost reached the outskirts of town when she realised that she had forgotten to pay the bill she had accrued at the bar. She knew that Scott would pay it, but she didn't want to be beholden to anyone.

Piper hadn't thought it was possible, but in the few weeks that she had been here, Piper had come to love most of the people here as if she had known them her whole life. Not only would it give her a chance to pay her bill, it would also give her a chance to say goodbye to her friends. She knew it was her way of putting off leaving, but an extra hour wasn't going to make a big difference.

Piper turned her car around and headed back towards the bar, feeling bluer then she had in weeks. She didn't want to leave this place or the people, but she had no choice, she was not ready to face Cameron yet.

When Piper reached the bar she parked her car and sat there for a while just looking at the place she had come to love. She still remembered her first time here, a small smile played at her lips to think of how far she had come from that rude woman who had flipped Scott and his friends off.

Knowing that putting it off was only making things worse, Piper took a deep breath, got out of the car and headed in.

"Hey girl how you going?" Susie asked from behind the bar as Piper walked in. "I didn't expect to see you until tonight."

"I'm good. Listen I know that we had plans to hang tonight, but I'm heading out, so I just wanted to drop by to say goodbye and pay out my tab."

Susie's face dropped and her eyes filled with tears. Piper had been expecting this reaction as over the past few weeks they had become close friends. From the first night Piper had met Susie she knew they would get on, and with Susie being new to town, it was only natural that the two of them helped each other settle in.

"Say it isn't so. I was just getting used to having a friend to hang out with. Now who am I going to have coffee with." Piper felt the same way, especially since her last friend had hurt her badly Piper appreciated the offer of friendship.

It was only through her friendship with Susie that Piper had begun to see the flaws that had been in her and Karen's relationship all along.

It was only just now that Piper realised that everything in their friendship had been about Karen. If the spotlight had not been on her, she was not happy. The time spent here had really done wonders for mending her outlook on life. And now Cameron had snatched that brief bit of happiness away, *again*.

"Oh God, now who am I going to hang with when all of the town events come up."

Tears filled Piper's eyes as she too thought about what she was leaving behind. But she had to go, she had no other choice.

"I am sure you will find someone to hang out with." Piper offered.

Susie came around the bar and hugged her friend.

"But they won't be you."

Piper let the tears fall once more. "I promise to keep in touch."

"I know but it's not the same." Susie let go of Piper and wiped the tears that had been falling.

"I know it won't. I would love to stay, truly I would, but something has come up and I have no option but to go."

Piper pulled out her credit card from her bag and handed it to Susie. Susie accepted it reluctantly and walked back around the bar to where she could put the payment through. Piper wasn't worried about using it now, the cat was out of the bag anyway, so she might as well use some of his money as well.

It didn't take long for Susie to put the order through and once the bill was paid, Susie came back around the bar and hugged her once more.

"Take care." Susie whispered.

"I will I promise. I will give you a call tonight when I get to my destination."

Piper let go of her friend and turned around to leave, tears once more in her yes. But, at the same time Scott walked through the door. Piper's feet became glued to the floor.

Piper's heart beat faster at the sight of the magnificent man before her, she wanted nothing more than to run to his arms, but the look on his face stopped her. Scott had such a serious look on his face that it gave her pause. She had never seen that look before. It was a look that could only mean one thing. Trouble!

"Darlin' we have to talk about this."

Piper was shaking her head. She knew what he was going to say, but she couldn't do it.

"Scott please don't make this any harder than it has to be. I can't stay here, I have to go. I told you when this thing started that there was to be no strings attached and you knew that." Piper didn't know who she was trying to convince him or herself.

As Scott watched her, his eyes softened and a small smile played at the edge of his lips. It was then that she realised that she was only trying to convince herself. He already knew what she was only just coming to terms with. Piper had done something stupid, she'd done the one thing she had made him promise not to do. Piper had become attached to him.

There was no way around it, she knew now that she loved this guy. Scott was everything that she wanted in a partner, in truth he was everything Cameron was meant to be. But Piper wasn't ready to trust anybody like that again, she wasn't ready to get her heart broken and on top of that, she knew it would never work as they came from different sides of the world.

Tears started flowing down her face. She didn't mean for them to come, but she couldn't help it. She noticed that Scott started to walk over to her, and she knew that the moment his arms touched her she would be powerless to stop her emotions.

Piper took a step back, put her hand out and shook her head. She hoped that Scott got the message and stopped. But when he continued to come towards her, she pleaded with him.

"Scott, please." But Scott being as stubborn as he had simply grabbed her and enveloped her in a hug. Piper let all her barriers fall and melted into his arms. She was through fighting, her world just felt right when she was in his arms. However, even though in this moment Piper felt safe she was worried that her emotions were playing tricks on her.

*What if he was just a rebound? What if Cameron was right and she was unlovable? What if Scott got sick of her the same way Cameron had?*

Doubt after doubt flooded Piper's mind and the worry that the feelings she had for him were just a knee-jerk reaction to what had happened were starting to take over. She didn't know if she could go through losing Scott the way she had lost Cameron.

"Darlin' please don't cry, I know you said no strings attached but I couldn't help it. I couldn't help falling in love with you."

Piper pulled back and looked him in the eyes. Piper almost lost herself in the honesty she saw in their blue depths, the warm of his hug and the smell of the country that he always seemed to wear. But her head was telling her to tread carefully. She had given her heart completely once before and it had almost ruined her.

"You, you can...nooot be in love with me, please do not say that" Piper pleaded in a whisper, even as her heart did a flip in her chest.

Piper waited for the Scott to renounce what he had just said. Piper had given him the out he needed. But confusion filled her as he shook his head and smiled.

"What am I going to do with you darlin?'"

Piper was a little annoyed at his question. Scott knew exactly why she couldn't accept what he had said. She when to pull away from him, but Scott wouldn't have it. He tightened his arms and kissed her head. Piper snuggled deeper into his arms and breathed him in deeply. She was just about to answer him when Scott started speaking again. Piper closed her eyes and teased the deep tenor of his voice as it rumbled through his chest to her.

"I know that you don't want to hear it, Piper, but you have to. You have become my heart and I refuse to let you go. I want you to stay and see if we can make this work. Please give us a go. I promise I will never ever hurt you the way he hurt you."

Piper was shaking her head again. Just the mention of her ex brought back all the broken promises he had made.

Cameron had promised not to hurt her the day they got engaged. He had promised to love only here, and he had promised to be the one person she could always count on. But look where she was standing. She'd been with Cameron for six years and he had turned to someone else once he was bored with her; he had broken every promise he had ever made, what would make Scott any different?

"Tell me that you feel differently. That in these past few weeks you felt nothing towards me. Tell me that what we had together *didn't* make you feel like your heart was melting."

Piper shook her head, she didn't want to do this.

"Please Scott, just let me go."

Even though Piper has said the words, she still held to Scott as though her life depended on it. She knew that her denial was hurting him, but she didn't know if she was brave enough to give him her heart. She expected Scott to give up, but when he pulled her back so that she could see his eyes, a small part of her wall started to fall. In his eyes Piper didn't see anger, or frustration, or even sadness. No there she saw determination.

"Alright Piper, if you can honestly tell me that you feel nothing for me, that over the past few weeks you haven't fallen in love with me I will walk away and let you leave."

Piper knew that she owed Scott and herself to consider what he was saying. Taking a step back Piper thought about how she was feeling, not just on the surface, but deep down inside of her heart.

Was she feeling angry? No not really.

Did she still want to kill Cameron? Well yeah of course, who wouldn't after what he had done.

But did she still *love* Cameron?

As these thoughts rushed through her head, the door swung open and as though her thoughts had conjured up the devil himself in walked her worst nightmare, Cameron!

## CHAPTER FOURTEEN

$\mathcal{N}$umb and exhausted, Piper could only stand and watch as he strolled towards her, and as he did she finally took note of the person he was, and the last question she had asked her played in her mind.

Cameron didn't take note of who was around him, he just had eyes for her. Piper wanted to run, she was not ready to face anyone, let alone the man who had cost her everything. Piper looked around the room trying to figure out what to do, that was when her eyes landed on Scott.

He still stood in front of her, but his look of love had been replaced with one of rage. Piper moved her eyes from Scott to see that Cameron wore the same expression he always wore when she wasn't doing what he wanted.

Normally that look made her feel guilty, but she found that the look only annoyed her now, she could see it for what it was. Cameron's way of making her feel less than she was. Scott had never worn that look, even when she wasn't doing what he wanted. Scott had never made her feel anything but worshiped.

"Piper! What the hell? I've been trying to find you for weeks now. Why would you just run out like that? you should have stayed so we could talk about it." Cameron's annoyed tone brought forward all of the anger that she had felt the day she walked in on him and Karen.

*Was he serious? Was he really asking her that? Was he in the same room that she had been?*

"Is this the moron that chose someone else over you?" Scott asked her, tension filled his voice.

Cameron finally stopped noticing that there was more people in the room than just himself and Piper. Cameron then looked at Scott who was now leaning against one of the tables not far from Piper. Piper could feel the tension building in the room. Cameron's body had stiffened, and even though Scott looked relaxed, Piper could tell from the way that this cheek ticked that he was anything but. She was not sure she was ready to deal with the fight that looked to be brewing.

Cameron tried to make himself look more intimidating. Scott simply raised one eyebrow.

*God could this get any worse?*

Piper was just about to tell them to cool it, when the realisation hit her. The last question that she had asked herself had finally been answered. While she had been standing her dealing with the anger that she felt for Cameron, she had failed to miss that there was no longer any love there. Piper narrowed her eyes and focused all of her energy on Cameron. She tried to block out everything else that had happened and only focused don him. Piper considered all of the emotions that were spiralling around inside of her, she noted that one was missing.

Love. There was no love left for Cameron.

As the realisation hit her, a huge smile broke out across her face. Piper looked at Scott, then Cameron, then back at Scott. She smiled at him to let him know everything was okay. Scott beamed back at her and the moment she noticed the tension leave his body, Piper knew that she no longer had to worry about a fight. All she had to worry about was getting Cameron out of here so she could figure out what she was going to do with her life.

Turning back to Cameron Piper prepared herself for the battle she knew was coming. Yeah, she was still angry at him and yeah, she still wanted to cut his nuts off for being a two-timing bastard. But all the affection she'd felt for him and all of the feelings that she'd had for him were gone, even the niggling doubt that had reared its head mere minutes before were gone.

Piper smiled as she came to terms with the knowledge that along with the doubt, her pain had also gone. Her affection and love were no longer attached to a man that made her feel as though she was unlovable, instead they were all firmly directed at Scott. All she needed now as time and privacy to fill him on her decision. Piper looked at Scott, as she did her heart beat a little faster and her pulse picked up as butterflies filled her stomach. Piper didn't know when it had happened, but the man in front of her had managed to mend her broken heart and make her feel as though she was worth loving. Piper couldn't wait to show him just how much that meant to her.

Cameron drew Piper's attention back to him when he spoke. "Piper, you have to listen to me, you have to come home. We can fix this, we can go to therapy. This was just a small bump in the road, it is not worth throwing six years of our life down the drain for. We can do anything you want, just come home please."

Piper didn't even feel a little bad for him, they'd been together for six years and he had ruined it. It was *his* choices that drove them here. He chose to sleep with Karen, he had made his bed, now he could sleep in it, alone... or with Karen, she didn't care anymore.

"No Cameron, I won't be coming home, not now or ever. It is *over*."

Piper took an involuntary step back as anger crossed his face. She had seen the look many times over the years and once more she was reminded of how different he and Scott were. Perhaps things happened for a reason, and as she continued to look at the man she had once loved, Piper was starting to see what her life would have been like and for the first time since she had walked in on Karen and Cameron she was glad for what had happened.

"It can't be over Piper; can't you give me another chance?"

Piper knew that they were playing this out in front of an audience, but she just didn't care. Thankfully she knew the people in this room were on her side. Piper looked around the room, Susie had moved off to give them some privacy. She was currently cleaning down tables, and even though she looked as though she wasn't paying any attention, Piper knew that Susie was listening to every word.

Piper smiled and was once more glad for the friendship they had. Her eyes fell on Scott next, he was still leaning against the table, and when he winked at her she smiled and knew she needed to finish this. Piper knew that she needed to get out all of the emotions that had caused her doubt over the past few weeks, especially if she had any chance of making things with Scott work.

"Yes, I can tell you it's over, and no I don't think you deserve another chance. You knew from the beginning of our relationship that cheating would be the one thing that would destroy us, and yet you still did it. What does that tell you? I'd like to know one thing though, was it just the one time, or had it been going on for a while?"

The pause was all the answer she needed.

"Goodbye Cameron."

"No Piper, please, it wasn't like that."

Piper had had enough, she couldn't listen to this anymore, she just wanted him to leave her alone. They both needed to move on.

Piper walked forward and put enough force in her tone to let him know that she was through talking "Just don't, Cameron, okay. You should've thought about our relationship and the consequences before you slept with my best friend." She could see that he was going to say something else, but Piper cut him short by placing her hand in the air. When she was sure that he wasn't going to say anything she continued.

"Look, there's obviously something between the two of you so I'm giving you my blessing to see where it goes. But don't expect me to have anything to do with either of you anymore. Our relationship is over, just know that I'm not gonna stand in your way. I'm not gonna be there anyway." Piper said the last bit for Scott's benefit, and the smile that spread across his face let her know that he understood what she had meant.

"What does that even mean, Piper?" Cameron asked.

Piper wasn't going to answer him, but then she thought better of it, she knew it would be the quickest way to get him to leave.

She walked over and placed herself into Scott's embrace, before she answered him. The moment his arms wrapped around her waist and he pulled her back so that her back was against his front she knew she was exactly where she was meant to be. His embrace gave her the strength she needed to finally let go of her past and except the future, no matter what it would bring.

"Well what it means is that I can honestly say that I've finally found something worth holding onto. It wasn't easy, as you broke my heart. And because of that I've been angry with the world. Because of that anger I almost missed a second chance at love. But I will not let you or anyone else keep me from what I deserve."

With that Piper turned around to face Scott. She was done with her past. It was time to start working on her future. She only hoped that Scott had meant everything he'd said earlier.

"Look, I'm not saying that I love you... not yet at least, and I'm not saying that we are going to be together forever, but what I am saying is that I would like to give this a go. There is definitely something here and I *have* enjoyed our time together. So, if the offer still stands I would like to stay."

Scott grabbed her and kissed her hard.

As their lips touched, Piper's world felt like it was right once more. And when she heard Cameron storm out of the bar slamming the door as he went, she couldn't even fathom up a little bit of regret that that part of her life was closed. Now it was time to open up a new chapter and see where it led her.

Piper just hoped that it would lead to her salvation.

# CHAPTER FIFTEEN

Five years later...

"Hey Pipes, can you come in here for a minute?" She heard Scott call from the living room. As she followed his voice, she saw him minus his shirt, with his head under one of the tables, fixing something. She loved watching him work as the sweat glistened off his chest and muscles as he worked.

"Hey babe, what do you need?"

"I just need you to pass me that tool over there, please darlin'."

Piper walked over to grab the tool he was pointing at and passed it to him as an idea hit her. Once he was pre-occupied with his task again, she lent down quietly, unbuttoned his jeans and slid them down over his hips.

"What are you doing, darlin'?" he asked his voice a little hoarser than it had been minutes ago.

"Trying to work! You?" Piper giggled at his grunt and continued to pull down his jeans to reveal his cock. Once she had it in her sights, she placed her mouth over it and started to pleasure him. She took him all the way to the brink and over. Piper smiled as she licked the last of his pleasure form the tip of his manhood, she loved the taste of him, and not even in the last five years could douse her desire for him.

Looking up at Scott she saw that his eyes were closed and he was just lying there, completely still. She smiled to herself. Even though they'd been married for four years out of the five they'd been together, she still loved that she could make him want her as much as he had the first day they had met.

As the years had passed by with Scott, Piper eventually realised that what she thought she'd had with Cameron was merely a memory of the young, lust-filled romance they'd had in school. It was not real and that was why he turned to Karen. He must've known it in his heart as well. Especially since only six months after he returned home, him and Karen had eloped. At first she had felt a little hurt that he had married the woman he had cheated on her with so quickly, but as her relationship with Scott had grown all of her pain and anger had disappeared and now she was pleased to know that everyone was finally with the people they were meant to be with.

She was also please to know that she never had to worry about Scott leaving her for someone else. Piper knew that he would never wander because every day he made love to her, and every day he let her know that she was needed. Even when she was on her archaeological digs, he went with her. They could not bear to be away from each other for long, and her and Scott's relationship was the kind of relationship she'd wanted all along. Piper now new that she had wanted, no needed, someone who loved her as much as she loved him. And Scott was that someone.

Just then a cry sounded from upstairs through the baby monitor.

"Oops, looks like little Jasper is awake. I'd better go get him," she said, rising from her position on the floor. Scott stood and righted his jeans.

"This is not over, darlin'," he growled as she headed upstairs.

"Oh, I agree, it's definitely not over, I expect some love later." she said winking at him before she rounded the corner into the hall.

Walking into the baby's room she picked up Jasper, and as her five-month-old son smiled at her, she knew that her life was complete, she knew that she had made the right decision coming to Alabama.

After all she had been through the country had been her salvation after all.


The End

97